Small Town Moments

CLEAN SMALL TOWN ROMANCE

MAPLEWOOD GROVE - VOLUME 1

DAISY LANDISH

BEACHES AND TRAILS PUBLISHING

BEACHES AND TRAILS
PUBLISHING

Sweet Rivals

Chapter One

ETHAN

"You're a *peach*, Ethan! Burger on the house today."

Ethan Parker aims a strained smile Loretta's way. "Don't mention it, ma'am," he grunts, lugging another carton from the bed of his pick-up truck. "It's no big deal."

"Oh, you've gotta learn to take a compliment, hon," Loretta tuts, swiping the back of her free hand over her slightly lined forehead. She slumps against the bare brick wall at the back of her diner. Ethan knows she'll never admit it, but she's getting up there in age. It felt immoral to watch her wrestle her deliveries down the street in her rusty stock trolley while driving by. Why no one else had stopped would bug him all day.

He shoots her a look. "And you've gotta stop giving food away on the house in this economy," he reminds her, passing by with the last of the boxes. It wasn't the first time that week he'd seen her do so—albeit, it had been more than two days since Loretta had last attempted it with him.

"I'll work on it if you will," she chirps.

Ethan isn't fooled for a moment. He'd lost count of how many iterations of this exchange they'd had by now. Loretta wouldn't change, and

3

neither would he. Fortunately, both of them could live with this normal of theirs. His fondness is unmistakable when his hand squeezes over the damp shoulder of her weathered white t-shirt. "Uh-huh."

"C'mon in for a drink," Loretta orders. Adding, just as his mouth opens to argue, "Don't sass me, boy. Marie'll make it."

His jaw snaps shut obediently. He may have been grown enough to summon the gall to sometimes argue with the diner owner. But she'd still, a lifetime ago, been his dad's pal. He wasn't around anymore. In the wake of that fact, Loretta Beam felt more maternal a figure than ever. She'd certainly been more present than Ethan's actual mother for a decade and counting. It made her family, something he appreciated in the ways he knew how.

He motions for her to go on ahead of him. "I wasn't going to *sass* you," he mutters eventually. "I was *gonna* point out that I'd been driving to the diner in the first place. I'm meeting the guys. Noah's in town this week, so we figured we'd swing a powwow before he's off and back to the city." Noah was one of his best friends, and he also happened to be Ethan's business partner and occasional roommate. He didn't remotely look the cutthroat corporate type, but he ran several businesses—one of which was Parker's Wrench, the auto repair shop Ethan's father had left him.

The diner owner hums in response, hip-checking him in passing.

Of course, she's a precious, plump, and squat little lady, that Loretta —and Ethan hulked over most at six feet and three inches. Her nudge lands somewhere near his thigh. Despite himself, Ethan snorts a short laugh. "Nice," he teases, earning a smack on his rear with a dishtowel he doesn't question her procurement of.

Swatting him away, she playfully admonishes, "*Shoo!*" Then, catching sight of his cluster of friends, she hollers, "*Noah Harrison!* You come and get your pal before his beverage privileges are officially revoked!"

Ethan's fingers rub over the small grin fighting the corners of his mouth. "A beverage she bestowed on me for being a *peach,* by the way," he divulges in lieu of a greeting to his best friend, who jogs up to the right side of the counter. Loretta's rag swats his arm this time, earning a sprawling smile.

Hands raised in defense, Noah says, "I believe Loretta over you any day, dude."

Ethan wouldn't expect any different. Shrugging easily, his palm splays over the countertop, bracing his weight for him to vault over it. His calves narrowly miss the row of maroon vinyl stools that line it.

"*Watch it,*" someone hisses behind him.

Ethan jerks back. *Yikes.* "Woah, sorry, ma'am- That's my b—" He's already apologizing before turning. Of course, the moment he does, he stops short. He knows he shouldn't have bothered. There was no point in wasting his breath. Whatever he said would go nowhere, judging by the ferocious glare etched into Olivia Wright's face. His very presence was all it took to summon it. Any further infractions on his part were only icing on the cake. Or blood on a shark's teeth, as it were. Olivia was no cake.

There was no escaping the fact, either. Unlike Loretta, she was taller than most girls in town. He wasn't sure of the exact measurements. But he knew she could meet his eye, and refused to do more than cant her sharp jaw to do it—the way she tips it now, uppity as ever. "Ma'am's my mama, thank you very much," Olivia snaps with enough gusto to knock a complicated-looking braid clean off her tan, sculpted shoulder. *Case in point,* Ethan thinks, brows crawling up his forehead.

"Hey, Liv!" Noah greets warmly over Ethan's shoulder.

For him, with a slight turn of her head, the shark relinquishes a crooked smile. "Hi, Noah," she drawls like Noah is her oldest of friends. Except he isn't. She didn't even know him six months ago, for the love of Pete!

It's frustrating that Ethan doesn't have to question its fakeness, either. He's come to understand she isn't the sort to fake anything, not for any reason. Even if she doesn't like him—and she didn't from the get-go, from their very first encounter when she arrived in town—he could still appreciate the authenticity. When she smiles, she does it with her whole face; it dimples her cheeks and brightens her eyes. Just as expressive in her affections as she was in her annoyance. Where Noah receives the former; the latter is all for Ethan. He's sure he doesn't imagine the peculiarly intense amber of her irises flashing like warning signs.

5

He's used to it by now. "All right, Olivia," he relents. Somehow, he resists pinching his nose's bridge before turning on his heel. He waves pointedly to Liam's overly amused face instead, leaving them to it.

Loretta's beverage sounds downright heaven-sent now.

Olivia

You can't be everyone's cup of tea. For most of her life, Liv had understood that well enough. She'd been reliably informed in the past that she showed a strength of character not to crave it. Growing up smack dab in the middle of a considerable brood, it didn't matter. No matter what, there would always be five siblings and two parents with the biological responsibility of accepting her. And they had. It made no sense, then, for Ethan Parker to still bother her.

Yet bother her he does.

In the face of it, it's Noah who earns her ire this time. He interrupts her scowling with his breezy chuckle effortlessly. Pearly white teeth flash in a boyish grin beneath an aquiline nose. She almost expects him to be chewing gum—to blow a bubble in her direction. He's perpetually Peter Pan that way. Usually, she appreciates that levity about him.

Confronted with Noah's unfortunate choice of best pal and business partner, however... It tends to make Liv unappreciative in general. That man, with his terse responses, inscrutable face, and a blank slate of a personality. His dismissive attitude had irked her from day one. Unlike her short fuse now, he couldn't blame it on a bad day. It's how Ethan always is: aloof and disparaging. No matter the occasion of a run-in, he is prone to treating her like she isn't good enough to waste conversation beyond clipped syllables.

Liv's bad day, meanwhile, directly correlates with his existence. She'd spent most of it dwelling on that fact. It's what she'll have to blame for not helping it when she sighs, "I don't get how someone like you is friends with someone like him."

Then again, it's a wonder to her, too, that Noah doesn't puff his chest and defend Ethan either. He shrugs instead, unbothered. "He's good people, Livvy," is all he says.

Noah wasn't the first to say so. She'd heard a version of it from Betty Lou, the first friend she'd made in Maplewood Grove. A little more dependably, she'd heard it from Loretta too—whom she'd also overheard telling Ethan to befriend her, just as she'd heard Ethan say, *I have enough friends, Lor.*

"Good doesn't mean nice," Liv grumbles bitterly.

Noah laughs again. "Livvy, you're not that nice either. But you're good people too."

As luck would have it, Noah Harrison was as hard to be annoyed with as a golden retriever puppy. This, coincidentally, is precisely what he resembled in Liv's eyes. It's without any heat that her jaw drops and her brows furrow. "*Rude!*" she gasps in mock affront, eyes rolling emphatically.

It's enough of a concession for Noah to electric boogaloo away from her, tossing her a wink. "Eat a donut, save a life," he advises sagely before he drops into the booth housing his best friends; Noah on one end and Liam Brooks on the other, sandwiching Ethan in. They're a spectrum in every way. Olivia doesn't keep watching.

No one would notice that she forgoes the donut in the end.

Truthfully, she doesn't have much of an appetite. She'd thought just being at Loretta's—immersed in delightful smells of richly fragrant coffee and buttery goodness—would be enough to rouse her spirits. And, for a moment, it had been. Just stepping inside the diner did that some days. A swish of a door, the greeting jingle of the bell. A smile from Loretta Beam that was always worthy of her last name. The scattered chorus of casual waves of hands and hellos. Some other days, though—like this one—it wasn't such an easy task.

There were days when it delighted Liv that this town was full of people, and she knew almost everyone by name now. Only a few months into being a Maplewood Grove resident, she knew her way around this town. Those days, she felt like she finally fit. It's as if she's been a lost puzzle piece floating through life in Nashville, Tennessee all this time when she'd really been meant to be here. In the house that her late grandmother Julia had left her. Right in the heart of this small town she'd fallen in love with as a little girl.

Today, standing in the diner where she had her dinner most evenings, Liv felt seen in the worst way. Oh, they knew her, that's for sure.

She was Olivia Wright—'Liv' to most. Twenty-eight years old. The granddaughter to Julia Wright. Julia had been a beloved Maplewood Grove native all her life. Liv lived in the house she'd inherited from her.

She was also a recent owner of *Fixed Wright Bodyshop;* a labor of love she'd invested her heart, time, and savings into.

There was no way they didn't all know it was failing. They all preferred *Parker's Wrench,* instead. Maybe they'd even seen her sitting in the empty workshop all day. Just watching time tick by, minute by taunting minute. Watching her glossy, unmarred tools that hadn't earned some grease in weeks. She was finding that shame was unique when there were spectators to it.

Growing up in a family as large as hers, Liv hadn't realized being *one of too many* could be a blessing, too. Now, she wished for the very invisibility she'd spent her adolescence resenting. Her pulse pounded in her ears. The baby hairs on the back of her neck stood at attention. She could practically *feel* their pity.

And she couldn't help but wonder—if not a donut, what else would fix this?

Chapter Two

OLIVIA

Some days, all you've got in your arsenal is taking a deep breath. Liv is more fortunate than that—when she lets herself be. Today, she makes herself. Or, more accurately, Betty Lou makes her. It's hard to fail at, walking through town to an impromptu town hall meeting.

The grass remains bright, summer green, but the air has changed. The weeks of running from one destination to another, dodging summer storms, have passed. Leaves have begun to crisp. Their edges darken with an impending fall's lingering stain. The storms will return soon enough, with handfuls of snow. In the meantime, she's helplessly enchanted by the clear sky and the honeyed glow it bathes the town in.

This is how she's always loved Maplewood Grove best: in transition. In its vibrant springs or its sentimental autumns, when the colors are so rich it makes her heart ache to think about too long. Liv is no poet—but sometimes she understands why others claim to be.

One of them walks right beside her, arm looped through Liv's, head ducked close and conspiratorial. "Oh, did I tell you that story—don't tell anyone I've told you, of course, since it's all *very* hush-hush, but just between us two—there's been *talk* that those Carlton dames just may have something not-so-innocent buried in the soil of those prize-winning roses of theirs. It's why their flowers are in such high demand. Give one to a suitor, and their heart is *yours*." Liv wouldn't necessarily call Betty Lou Hopkins a *poet*... But with her dramatic gold ringlets, big blue eyes, doll's mouth, theatrical diction, and sensational stories, one couldn't deny her stage presence. Even if that presence was currently being channeled into gossip about the intriguing Carlton twins, Agnes and Mabel, both of whom were well into their 70s.

At least she does it with flair, Liv allows, biting back a laugh. But she doesn't want to laugh at Betty. No matter what anyone else said—and *everyone* seemed to have plenty to say—the blonde had already proven to be Liv's friend. Sympathetic and sweet, Betty cared. She'd cared enough to be the one to ring Liv's landline that morning and demand Liv take a walk with her. She'd ignored Liv when she'd tried to beg off the communal gathering.

A little fresh air and people-watching can do wonders for the soul, Betty had cooed down the line. And she had been right.

Liv feels it; she feels lighter and more solid at the same time. Especially halfway into the mocha latté her friend had brought along on her walk over to Liv's door. To think, Olivia hadn't even told Betty Lou that she'd been avoiding Loretta's the past few weeks. She definitely hadn't explained why. She finds herself unable to muster suspicion. The warm, silent swell of gratitude occupies too much room. It had made her feel seen and cared for, for Betty to have noticed. It's siphoned away her loneliness like a vacuum cleaner taken to crumbs.

Her best friend back in Nashville would call her a soft touch. Liv would tell her to hush. She'd tell Ellie she has a *Rep to protect*. Except she didn't, really. Not in Maplewood Grove. And hadn't that been the point of her big move to this little town in upstate New York?

A new beginning. One that was truer to herself than her past had been. It was supposed to have been an easier feat than it was turning out to be. Smoother, somehow. Less stressful.

So what if it hadn't been what she'd imagined it would be? Little in life was. Olivia was many things, and not all of them complimentary— but she'd never been naive. Out of the house that was filled with memories of a grandmother who was gone now, and an empty workshop that had been haunting her with its unnatural silence, Liv grapples for perspective. She looks around the Sip 'n Saw bar with its wood fixings and red, white, and navy decor. People chatter good naturedly around her, like neighbors in wholesome '90s sitcoms.

"Hey-ah, Liv!" a voice sounds to her left. She whips around, and her surprise splays across her features obviously enough for her to know it. Still, she waves back to Loretta before she and Betty take their seats in the middle of the throng.

Why had she been so sure they'd forget she existed if they didn't see her? More people greet her. Ask her if she'd been feeling under the weather. Asking her if she's good now. Betty Lou looks at her, toting a smug grin. The squeeze of her hand around Liv's arm is a *See, I told you so!* she allows.

Ethan

Ethan isn't likely to admit it aloud, ever—but a part of him enjoys these town meetings. A part of him that respects the tradition of it all; the almost ridiculous ceremony of it all. He could script it himself, he imagines: from Mayor Beckett's loud tie to the elderly Carlton twins' bickering to Dot Simmons taking charge. It may not be normal to everyone. But it's been his normal all his life. Where there's plenty about his stock in life that keeps Ethan up some nights, these meetings aren't one of those things.

They remind him of his dad, sure. It isn't in a bad way. He found just as much humor as Ethan in it all. Maybe it's the time that has gone by that's made it all easier. Maybe it's that his oldest friend Liam, who had been by his side since either of them could really talk, and Alex, who was a great cousin and an even better pal, flank him on either side.

"You checking out Dot again, you perv?" Liam elbows his side, snickering.

On his other side, Alex replies, "Always is. Can't blame him. She's too powerful to resist. Little weird since she dated his dad once upon a time—but I guess bros don't shame. The heart wants what it wants..."

Ethan swiftly takes back every nice thing he's just thought about them. Guffawing, he flicks the backs of both their heads. "You're gross. Shut up."

Liam whispers loudly, "*Yeah*, Alex, shoot. He's trying to listen to Dot! Respect, dude."

While his cousin laughs soundlessly but too hard to reply, Ethan deadpans, "I hate you both. Just thought you should know that."

"We know," Alex chokes out, nostrils flaring and lashes wet.

A pointed cough sounds from speakers scattered all around the bar. Their heads snap to the podium where a willowy brunette stands on a stage behind a podium, looking right at them. Not accusatory so much as she is intimidatingly distinguished. Dot has that way about her. Her blouse is black and it matches the reading glasses perched at the tip of her nose; her mouth is unsmiling, but her eyes are swimming with mirth. "If you're finished, boys," she announces into the microphone staidly, "should we get on with business?"

Ethan grins smugly, miming applause. Dot, without a reaction he wasn't expecting her to dignify them with in the first place, moves on. There is a stack of papers in front of her. She taps its edges out without rifling through them.

"This isn't likely to come as a surprise to anyone. It's that time of the year, guys. We're here to get the ball rolling on this year's fall fair." There's a murmur of agreement that spreads through the crowd. Dot pauses for it, then continues. "As you all know—" she casts a significant glance to the other side of the room, "—we lost a real pillar of our community earlier this year. The spectacular Julia."

Ethan's smile disappears quicker than it had formed. At just the mention of a name, his eyes seek her out of their own volition. *Liv.* Amidst all the bad blood between them blurring things, he'd almost forgotten what had brought her to town. The realization twists his guts like spaghetti around a fork. It's hard not to feel like an ass, catching sight of Olivia's typically fiery features shuttered and dimmed. He dislikes the bleak ghost of a smile she attempts. It's one he recognizes intimately. He doesn't grasp how far he's spaced out until he tunes back into Dot asking, "—anyone interested in taking up that mantle?"

He doesn't mean for his hand to shoot up.

If the look on Liam's face—torn somewhere between horror and amusement—is one to go by, so is anyone who knows him. It becomes the look he borrows when Liv's voice nearly bellows from the other side of the room, projecting when her body shoots up from her seat like an arrow: "*I'll do it!*" Her eyes zero in on him with a ferocity he is, in a word, *bewildered* by.

He's too taken aback to glean any pleasure from the way Dot's jaw drops, too. In front of everyone and their grandmothers. "Well— Er," she grapples, brows hitched halfway up her gently lined forehead. "Right. Uh, anyone else?" Ethan is at least 98% sure Dot asks to buy herself time to process. There is no way she doesn't know that it was asking for trouble, throwing him and Olivia Wright on the same team.

The woman, to put it *kindly,* had it out for him. To put it truthfully? She hated his guts. Vocally. At every turn. She had since he'd pissed her off all the way back in February—which happened to be the first time he'd ever met her. It feels like a foggy dream he's remembering, thinking of her walking into his garage shaking flurries out of her hair.

She'd ripped a dark green beanie off her head, just to mess her hair up in an attempt to smooth it. He had stared dumbly while she'd plucked snowflakes out of long lashes casting crescents on her high cheekbones, like a kid about to make a wish. Right after, she'd told him hiring her would be the best choice he'd ever make. He'd said he didn't need help. Because he *hadn't*. She'd puffed her chest and announced he did; he just didn't know it yet. He vaguely remembered his exhaustion. It felt so distant, telling her that an ego that big needed earning.

It had been the first time she'd glared at him. The last time she'd smiled at him, too—or so he'd thought till last week. Till he sees her now, her teeth bared. Apparently, she can do both at the same time.

Ethan drags a hand through his hair, roots burning. She isn't interested in anything he has to say. He knows it, and she knows it. So, what good was this going to do? His incredulous gaze drags its way back to the podium. But Dot doesn't look winded anymore. She looks... Thoughtful. He watches on as she says, as if in slow motion, "Okay. Liv Wright and Ethan Parker will be co-chairs heading the committee. Venue will, as always, be Maple Grove. Proceeds will be divided between housing, maintenance, and the school. Responsibilities include everything from vendors to games to safety precautions and decorations. Please come see me after the rest of the meeting and I'll... show you both the budget allowances and previous vendors who are happy to contribute again this year." She gives a decisive nod.

Ethan doesn't question why he imagines a nail being pounded into a coffin.

Chapter Three

OLIVIA

It isn't lost on Liv, that in all the time she's known him, she and Ethan Parker have never *planned* to meet. Their run-ins have been an outcome of providence. Or the Universe's sense of humor.

Today, it's different.

It's approaching twilight outside—and Liv lied to him and told him to pick her up after work. A lie, because she has nothing to work on. Or, at least, she isn't working on what she'd led him to believe she's working on. "*Ugh,*" she groans to the mirror. Even her reflection looks vaguely guilty. Any and all reminders to stow that guilt—to mark it as unnecessary—go ignored. Even seriously sitting down to be productive about fall fair business doesn't assuage the voice in the back of Liv's head that sounds suspiciously like her mama. It's very inconvenient.

But it jerks an astonished giggle out of her when Ethan, standing beside the passenger door, throws his hands up the moment she stomps down her stoop stairs. She couldn't explain what it is about the way he asks the sky, "*What* could I *possibly* have done to piss you off already?" All she knows is, it's hilarious. She also decides Ethan Parker might be kinda unhinged.

"Hello to you too, Scrooge," Liv drawls, humor unearthing her Southern twang.

"Me?" Ethan demands, eyes comically wide. "*I'm* Scrooge?"

Liv hums in agreement. "You're the one havin' a fit, Parker, jeez. All I did was walk over. To your car. Where you're waiting? So we can go sign up vendors? Like we agreed on yesterday. Did you hit your head or somethin'? Is any of this ringing any bells?" She waves her hand in front of his face—only partly facetious. Somewhat concerned. Mostly on the edge of laughing.

Her breath fissures when he snatches her wrist out of the air. His brows raise expectantly. Liv is aware she is staring, agog. "Do you ever shut up?" Ethan asks, not unkindly.

"'Fraid not," Liv answers honestly.

She watches him nod to himself. Quiet, like he's critically plotting a chess move. Until he asks, "So you're not about to snap at me?" He sounds unsure. Almost perplexed. Definitely rattled.

Liv could feel bad for him. She would, if he weren't a misogynistic jerk who'd been badmouthing her work ethic around town, and subsequently derailing her livelihood. But it is what it is. So, all she allows is an exasperated, "Do you want me to?"

"No," he's quick to say. "Then why does your face look like that?"

"Like *what?*"

"Olivia."

It's her mother's fault. It is totally and *completely* her mother's fault she blurts, "Because I *lied*. Man, I lied! Fine? *Happy?* I wasn't working. I've been watching the clock all day like a big fat loser and I said seven so *you'd* be done working because *you* have customers!" She practically spits the words out. Mortified, she thinks some may have actually landed on his shirt. "You know, it's rude to say things about someone's face. It's not like I can take it off and buy a new one. I'm not a Kardashian!"

Ethan

If it's even possible, Ethan is more confused than ever. He seems to have pressed a detonation button on her. Previously, he had believed this was a button he'd grown familiar with. As it turns out, Liv has more than one. He has her wrist in his grasp—and he isn't thinking when he squeezes it gently. "I know," Ethan says softly.

Olivia's face floods with color. Not until this very moment does he realize that she, *Olivia Wright,* isn't in her perpetual uniform of shorts, muscle tee, and bright red Sketchers. She's in a dress. A deeply red dress. With its hem down to her knees and big, tulip-like sleeves that cinch at her wrists. One of which he'd been holding before he'd coaxed her into his truck. There is gloss coating her lips. His fingers draw distressed circles against his temple. "I may have overreacted just now," he says, mostly to himself.

"*May,*" she mocks him. She pitches her voice higher than his had ever been, even before it dropped. She can't help herself, can she? Yet he doesn't point out that she's the one who seems to be having a total mental breakdown. He prefers her troublesome over troubled.

He nearly coughs out, "You look nice?" He doesn't mean for it to be a question, but it is.

He realizes how bizarre it is that he is comforted when she rolls her eyes at him. "Weirdest compliment ever, Parker."

"I didn't mean for it to be," Ethan says, his tone shifting from light to serious. "You just don't look... usual." The word feels inadequate, and he wishes he could take it back, seeing how she processes his words.

But then she shrugs it off. "My mama taught me to make a good impression, always. It makes it harder for people to say no to you."

As she comes back to her own factory settings, Ethan feels tension unwind in *his* belly, just watching the disconcerting panic in her features dissipate till her eyes are gleaming with her quintessential fire again. Only then does he step back, dropping the wrist he hopes she'll forget he was holding, and pulls open the tricky passenger side door. "Who could say no to those eyes?"

It is then that Ethan discovers something indispensable: Olivia Wright did, occasionally, shut up. You just had to shock her. He makes it all the way around the hood of the truck, and into the driver's seat before she's functioning again.

Even then, she's slow to quip, "Just drive."

Well, she supposes it's good to know she isn't the only one who is profoundly weirded out by Ethan opening her doors. Every single one of the people meeting them there—who had signed up to be vendors the night before—gapes at them.

But here they are.

She doesn't miss the irony of him holding the door to Loretta's diner for her. To think, it hadn't been a fortnight since she'd fled this very establishment. All for her to now walk in with the reason why.

"Let me guess," Ethan rumbles just behind her, "you're making fun of me in your head."

Liv can't deny she enjoys confounding him. She attaches no explanation when she disagrees, "No. Myself, actually. And you thought I was the one with the ego." Like a disapproving mother hen, she clucks her tongue at him. It's strange to her, too, the difference a twelve-minute car ride can make. Olivia almost forgets they aren't friends. If only she could forget why. He pulls out her chair anyway. "It's *Southern* hospitality, you know," she stresses, lips twitching with amusement.

"You can pull out my chair if you're dying to," Ethan allows.

"I'll show you pulli—"

Cliff Barnett's voice is like a bear's growl. Deep and gnarled. Extra disconcerting when he interjects, skepticism sharpening his syllables, "Aren't you two nemeses or whatever the hell it is the kids are saying these days?"

Liv nearly flinches. Immediately, she feels bad about it. It isn't his fault he looks and sounds dangerous. Cliff had kind eyes and a good heart. Anyone who met him could tell. He was just disconcerting when he wasn't directly being looked at, is all. Something she stops doing when Ethan nudges her ankle beneath the table.

One of the Carlton twins blows a noxious plume of smoke in their direction. "We've been waiting, darlings. Will you be requiring our services this year?" one begins. "*Or not?*" the other finishes.

"Yeah!" Liv is quick to exclaim, blinking owlishly. "I'm sorry—but which one of you is which? I have twin siblings. 'Course, they're harder to mix up because they're fraternal and different genders, but, surely the twin connection buys me some one-time brownie points?"

She finds it more than a little spooky, that both of them blink back in identical rhythm. Betty Lou may have been onto something with the witchcraft allegations. Her eyes narrow, like she'll see only one of them if she picks the right angle for it. "One is Mabel. One is Agnes. I know *that*. I'm right. Right?" she prods more. It's the other twin who blows smoke in her direction this time. Liv hadn't even seen a cigarette in her slightly tremoring, extremely wrinkled hand.

"Choose which," one says ominously.

"And we'll reward you with one of our roses," the other finishes.

Liv wonders if this is what Aladdin felt like, confronted by Genie. She can feel her entire face scrunch up. "Are they—? They're not. Betty's pulling my leg. She's got to be. There's no such thing as magical roses. This isn't some messed up Sleeping Beauty!"

That's all it takes for both twins to burst into identical hacking laughter. Liv is mildly concerned someone's dentures are going to pop out of their mouth and skip across the table like a pebble on the surface of a lake. "Doll, you know your grandma *never* would've fallen for that," one of them chortles. Her spittle rains from between her dry lips. The other grins a gummy smile. "But at least you've got her eyes! That'll get you some of our *magic* roses. You wanna give one to Ethan?"

In her periphery, she can feel Ethan shaking with laughter. Without looking at him, she kicks at his shin in retaliation. She knows she got him when he grunts back.

The look he must shoot is dirty enough for Cliff to mutter, appeased, "Nemeses-adjacent." Liv supposes it's as good a descriptor of their current status as any.

Ethan watches as Olivia acclimates to them. It isn't slowly. It isn't lost on him that it's remarkable, that it takes Liv a matter of minutes. *Minutes*, before they're laughing with her instead of at her. It's fascinating, the way she goes from defensive and dubious to giggling away with the batty old Carlton twins in real time.

He quietly slurps down his iced tea and eventually moves onto refilling bottles of ketchup for Loretta in the background when it gets harder to keep sitting in one place. He doesn't have to guess to know: if he hadn't been born into Maplewood Grove, it would've taken him an eternity to get these people to like him.

If he managed it at all.

He doesn't see a point in telling Liv he only signed on so she wouldn't have to. It seems to power her, having a project. He watches her smooth-talk Agnes and Mabel to agree to judge a contest. Listens to her corral Cliff into contributing his efforts towards setting up a karaoke stall. She even relinquishes a true blue laugh when Ethan makes her promise she won't get on that stage, for the greater good that was the town's hearing abilities.

She's whipsmart. Innovative. Cocksure, too—but it doesn't look so detrimental now. Something shifted. *What?* He doesn't understand.

Yet, dropping her back off at her door, Ethan can't shake the feeling it is a very different Olivia Wright that he drives away from at the end of the night.

Chapter Four

OLIVIA

Long before signing up for a degree in Engineering, Liv had grown acquainted with the basic law of gravity. It was simple: *What goes up, must come down.* It was always the simple things one forgot, wasn't it? Nearly a full week of feeling good about herself—of having faith in her abilities again—and something must come crashing down.

The past few days had gone by smoothly. Mabel and Agnes, delightful and dynamite a duo, had turned out to be even chattier than Betty Lou. It hadn't been an insidious mission to charm them. Liv hadn't known what to expect with them at all. Still—charm them, she had. Enough that they'd been singing her praises around town. It must have been praises they meant, too, since they also find her hunched over working on the Carlton twins' lawnmower, of all things.

Some business, though, sure beats no business. Olivia held fast to that mantra.

Then, in the middle of the afternoon, her phone rings. Still tinkering with the machine, her thumb distractedly swipes grease over her screen in her rush to answer. She doesn't catch the caller ID. If she had, maybe she would've gifted herself a moment of gathering her composure.

Surely there could be no *good* reason her main decor supplier was calling her in the middle of the day, the day he was supposed to be en route with the supplies. If there was, her supplier wasn't going to be the one to supply it.

"I'm very, *very* sorry, Miss Wright. It's a backend production issue," he prattles in her ear. There's more, and she can't process it. Liv grasps the gist of it. That's enough to have anxiety prickling beneath the knobs of her spine.

They're supposed to start setting up the marquee *tonight,* she thinks. Her chest aches, her skin suddenly too tight over her bones. She feels like it's shrinking, her skin morphed into a garment left swirling too long on a hot water cycle. Her heart beats too loudly in her ears. Pounding *thud, thud, thud.* An angry fist against a shut door.

She almost whacks Ethan in the face with a wrench before she sees him. Even then, he saves himself. Right at the last moment, he ducks. She doesn't know what he's doing here. But she doesn't have it in herself to question it either. Her efforts pour into wheezing out, "*No- Decorations-*" She can't even spare the embarrassment when her eyes burn. Her vision blurring. Her fists curling by her side, almost refusing to relinquish the wrench Ethan manages to pry out of her hand. "I can't believe this is happening."

"There's always a way," he insists. Liv almost itches for her wrench back—needing to do something with her suddenly empty hands. She thinks better when her hands are busy. It's how she's always been. It's why she's good at this. Maybe what she isn't is a planner.

"I should've just let you done this. What the hell was I thinking? I'm not a *planner,*" she bursts, pacing away from him. She doesn't care if she looks unhinged. She might as well. She feels about a million times worse.

Ethan

Olivia sounds close to tears, and Ethan doesn't know what to do with it.

He wasn't a vain man—in fact, his dad had sternly raised him to be the opposite—but he couldn't help but wonder if it was him who was to blame for her unravelling. It was only the second time in all the time he'd known her (granted, *all the time* consisted of less than seven months) he'd made the conscious choice to spend time with her, and both times, it quickly dwindled to her frantic, eyes crazed.

He wasn't a whimsical, spontaneous man. Yet here he was, showing up at her shop unannounced. Part of him wants to wait for her to vanish in a puff of smoke. But he can't stomach leaving her like this, her fists quivering at her sides. "—Liv, can you please just sit down?"

There's a slightly crazed look to her eyes when her head shakes. It helps that she's present enough to add, "I deal better in motion. With crises. I'm panicking. I don't deal well with failure." She relays it simply, robotically, as though she were a detached medical professional relaying symptoms.

He processes that for a beat, wrenching the past away from the present like gummy candy stuck together, needing to be separated to be shared equally. Slowly, he nods. Clears his throat. "Okay, but... You haven't failed. We have time. We have people who'll help. There isn't always another way, but sometimes there is. Failure is several paces away. Come back." Ethan doesn't mean for his face to take on the expression it does. But he sees it in the reflection in an idling motorcycle's mirror: It's the same stern face his dad used to make when imparting advice. He barely reels back a grimace at the sight of it. He's quick to turn away.

"You just—" he tries, motioning for her to stay. Needlessly, since she doesn't seem to be planning to flee anywhere. "Let me make a phone call. Noah'll know what to do."

Ethan had felt stupid saying it, and he shouldn't have. There was a reason the man was at the top of his Favorites list.

There weren't too many glorious lessons Ethan had learned in his thirty-two years on Earth. Most of them, he fully believed, he could've done without. But Ethan knew this without a shadow of a doubt: Noah Harrison's dependability wasn't one of those lessons. He knew he could count on Noah because years of friendship had taught him he could. There may have been many times in life where Ethan had fallen flat on his face. There had been zero since he'd walked into his dorm room freshman year, finding a boy sprawled on a bare mattress like it was the beach, that Noah hadn't helped him back up.

No matter how uncertain he feels about Liv, not knowing what to do with her in the least, his gut knew Noah would. Liv was panicking. The sight of it alone made Ethan skittish—made him twitchy in ways he didn't respect about himself. *That's when you call for back-up,* he could almost hear Noah say before even reaching for his phone. It was one of the many privileges of honoring a chosen brotherhood for nearly two decades.

"Just come to the city, bro," Noah says jovially over the phone. He sounds like he doesn't have a care in the world. It had no reflection on the truth; that's just who Noah was. He knew how to laugh, and he didn't sweat the small stuff. Most things, to Noah, were the small stuff. "It's only a three-hour drive. Just shoot me the list." He breathes so easily, that Ethan winds up feeling ridiculous for being so tightly wound.

He considers handing the phone over to Olivia, too, for Noah to work his magic—but thinks better of it. After all, Liv wasn't him. And, while his anxiety was absorbed from her, hers was rooted in something deeper he didn't understand. As Ethan strides back into her garage, a single brow raises at the sight of her hunched back over what looks like a *lawnmower.* He considers Liv carefully, taking her moment of sufficient distraction to consider the best way to *not* accidentally detonate her again.

Somehow, he winds up offering: "Noah has a supplier in New York. Come on—I'll let you drive the truck."

Olivia

It's too soon to say he fixed it, Liv tells herself, readjusting in the driver's seat yet again. This time, she doesn't pretend it isn't because she can feel him watching her. There's a very specific way that Ethan does it. It's almost like... Like he's waiting for something. She can't decide what, though. She absolutely won't be asking him. *You should at least thank him,* a voice in the back of her head reminds. Like she doesn't know it. Like she hasn't considered it—and decided, *very* pragmatically, if she may say so herself, to not be so quick on the trigger. Wait and get to New York. See the decorations. Sign off on... whatever it is that must need to be signed off. And then. Right? Thank yous came after. *How about a thank you for staying when he didn't have to?* The voice edges, and Liv savagely bats it away, blinking hard, forcing her focus on the road ahead.

"Are you aware you're glaring at the windshield?" Ethan asks conversationally. "If you were an X-Men, some serious glass-shattering action would be happening right about now."

"*That,*" Liv says emphatically, "might be the nerdiest crap you've ever said to me."

She can hear him smiling. She doesn't know how. She just—does. She doesn't know what to do with that any more than she knows what to do with the niggling desire to smile back. As if this situation warranted a single reason to.

Apropos of nothing, Ethan tries again. This time, he remarks: "You haven't let Julia's flowers die." It isn't remotely a smart decision on his part. Whatever she'd been expecting him to say next—and she didn't know what that was, only that she'd expected him to try again—it hadn't been about her late grandmother. She nearly swerves them off the road from the sheer shock of it.

Her head snaps to the side so harshly, the side of her neck throbs in protest. Liv isn't deterred by it. Dubiety distorting her voice, she questions, "You know about my gram's flowers?"

The corners of his mouth quirk slightly. "I do. It's Maplewood Grove. Everyone knows everyone... I run in the morning. Things get noticed."

Liv nods to herself, trying to process that. Envision it, maybe. It wasn't hard to imagine him running, of course; he looked it. All his shirts, cotton or flannel, were weathered enough material that it all clung to his body. He was too chiseled to not work at it. Even his jawline is sculpted when Ethan looks away, giving her the moment. He just bides his time, waiting, waiting, waiting until she finally says, "I keep hearing how awesome she was. And she was. But I didn't know her anymore. She still left me her house—and I don't even know why. I have *five* other siblings."

"I didn't know that," Ethan says. It feels wrong to take a fact without sharing one, so he offers back, "I'm an only child. My parents got divorced when I was fourteen. Mom left. Got remarried. She lives in New York with her husband now. Tony."

"Oh," Liv exhales to the windshield. She isn't glaring anymore. "I... haven't been back here in years. You know, you get busy. I graduated, I got a job, I—" When she glances over at her pause, she finds him already watching her. She swallows before she forces herself to look back on the road. Eventually, she finishes: "It's funny. I didn't see myself as a person with regrets. I really didn't. I'm a cocksure, by-the-seat-of-my-pants, all-in kinda gal. Or I was. I *thought* I was. Turns out, I didn't know that I realized how little I liked my life until a random lawyer—who refers to his one-person firm with an *And Associates*, by the way—called me and dangled a carrot in front of my face. Next thing you know, I'm here." There doesn't seem to be anything else to do but shrug. It's his turn.

"The carrot in this case is the four-bedroom house Julia left in your name?" Ethan checks.

Liv chokes on a giggle. She allows a nod, still not looking at him. "You're a lot like her," Ethan chooses that moment to tell her. "I could see her leaving her home to someone who'd appreciate it. It's all she really had to give. We're not a town of billionaires, Liv. There's a reason I'm so protective of the shop. It's all my pops had, and it's all he left me. I get it."

"I noticed," she murmurs. Something inside of her settles in the quiet between them; the tension no longer like an elastic band pulled taut. Liv even manages to be nice and quiet for a few more seconds after. It's almost long enough to lull Ethan into a false sense of security—if he doesn't know any better.

Then, she pounces, her palm thumping against the steering wheel to punctuate every exclaimed, "*Woah, woah, wait–*" She doesn't bother to fight the mad grin that takes over her face. "Ethan, do I want to know why you know how many bedrooms my grandma had in her house? Gosh. How do you even know that?"

Ethan sighs deeply. "People really need to stop questioning my knowledge."

"Who else is questioning you?" Liv gasps, too delighted at the prospect.

He purses his lips and resolutely refuses to answer. Instead, he turns up the dial of the radio. And if, when she starts singing at a pitch surely only dogs can hear, she can tell the corners of his mouth are tempted to rise... then that's no one's business at all.

Definitely not hers.

Chapter Five

ETHAN

"—Thank you." It's such a delicate expulsion of air Liv releases the words in, Ethan almost believes he dreamt it. He must wear the confusion blatantly. A heartbeat later, she repeats, forcefully, "*Really.* Thank you, Ethan." Before he can say another word, her lips press to his cheek —and then she's gone. He dully registers the sound of her front door closing behind her.

Standing on the sidewalk in the middle of town, he doesn't know what to do with his hands. So, he shoves them into his pockets, as deep as they'll go. With a solid thwack, his back meets the side of his truck. The support is needed. Ethan stares at nothing at all, trying to piece together his recollection of the day. But it was all so tangled. A tangled web of nothing he'd expected this day to turn into when he'd rolled out of bed that morning. A day that he hadn't seen coming, back in a city he hadn't been back to since his dad had passed away. That had been nearly a decade ago, now. Somehow, it had been filled with laughter. Hot cider in Noah's swanky city apartment, where Liv had endlessly made fun of his furnishing choices and his absurd sunglasses collection. She'd unbraided her hair before driving both hands into the thick, glossy mass of it. When she'd shaken it out, it had smelled like lemons and coconut.

Ethan thinks he can smell it, still.

"Ummm, *dude?*" Noah's head pops out of the rolled-down window. "Did she just—?"

"Yeah," Ethan confirms, dazed.

Olivia

Nothing is perfect, and Liv wakes up with a smile on her face anyway. Just sitting up in her bed, her eyes catch on the darkwash denim jacket slung over the back of her vanity chair. Her toes curl against her sheets. With her eyes closed, she could almost feel Ethan's knuckles brush against her nape when he'd wrapped his jacket around her shoulders.

Dragging herself out of bed, though, meant she could be on her way out the door soon enough. So she does—rolling sideways and landing on her feet like an Olympian who'd stuck the landing, arms thrown in the air like she's awaiting applause. She feels that big, today. It was going to be a good one, Liv had decided.

Confidence propels her forward. When she dresses, she does so quickly. A pair of weathered jeans she wouldn't mind getting dirty, her favorite *Ramones* t-shirt, a pair of thick-soled boots, and Ethan's jacket. She tucks her phone in her back pocket, grabs a crisp Granny Smith apple, and then she's out the door. Liv doesn't bother making her way towards the auto shop. Both Liv and Ethan had been in quick agreement last night: they would be spending all day setting up. His pals would help. It would be like pre-gaming for a party they were throwing. Sipping cider and giggling through numerous video games on Noah's massive TV yesterday, Ethan had already Facetimed and recruited a sizeable brigade to do the heavy lifting.

Because of him, no anxiety needles at her when she strolls through town. There's a pep to her step and a hum between her lips. She doesn't think she's felt this much levity since she'd first driven into town. It's with that same idealism that she perceives Maplewood Grove now—aglow in a wonderful morning, with the sun out but an autumnal chill nipping at her cheeks.

It means something to her, that she gets to Maple Grove and he's already right there. More disheveled than she is and gorgeous for it. With the sleeves of his flannel button-down rolled over strong forearms while he heaves up tables to put them into equidistant spots that will become stalls over the course of the day. Liv doesn't approach Ethan yet.

For the moment, she's content just watching him work. It doesn't matter that she's never been the kind of woman who enjoys being wrong. She understands that she'd been wrong about Ethan now, and it was a lesson she didn't mind. He taught it to her with grace and generosity. He'd done it when he made her feel like one of his friends, including her when he could've just as easily taken the trip to Noah alone and helped her all the same.

Instead, he'd given her his keys and let her have the control she needed to feel grounded. He'd understood her—from her fear to her grief—and he'd respected her enough to talk to her about it. It feels so distant, the affront and pride she'd felt only a few weeks ago. Whatever it is that she feels for Ethan now, Liv doesn't have a name for it.

But, as she hoists up a bag of art supplies—paintbrushes, paint, glitter, and countless leaf-shaped paper cutouts—she knows she wants to come up with one with him.

Ethan

"You wanna talk about it yet?" Liam prods for the umpteenth time that morning, since Noah, the traitor, had unceremoniously spilled the beans. Like a giddy teenager who just couldn't hold it in, Noah had gushed the moment he'd seen him, undeterred by Liam's bug-eyed disbelief. Now, Noah is napping peacefully on the sofa in Ethan's living room. Meanwhile Ethan gets to grapple with *this*. This, being...

"Oh, bro, you can't even stop looking at her." Liam sounds vaguely awed. "Scout's honor, man? I never thought I'd see the day." Ethan hadn't either, but he doesn't want to say it. It feels like admitting something he doesn't want to believe about himself.

His silence does the opposite of de-escalating Liam. "What, is it the only way you could think of to defeat your great and terrible nemesis?"

"Yeah, you got it, man." Ethan sniggers at the preposterousness, shaking out a sheet to splay over the top of another table. "This is all actually part of my mastermind scheme to oust Olivia from this town. You know, she's insane, and any other way to try to talk to her results in her crying, so this is it. I'm going to charm away her hostility."

He's waiting for Liam to slap his arm and laugh back. Instead, he's met with silence. Only it isn't a weightless one. It isn't one where Liam's simply wandering off. No, he can feel her behind him—if nothing else, by now, Ethan knows what anger feels like, radiating off of Liv's body. Sure enough, there she is. Her lips press into a flat line. He doesn't realize he's bracing himself for her to explode till she steps back from him instead. Her head shakes.

The sound that leaves Liv might be the worst sound he's ever heard. Such a hollow, mirthless sound, and it's dressed like a laugh. But none of Liv's warmth rages in it. It's brittle and cold. Leaving him with it, she walks away.

Chapter Six

OLIVIA

Wrath and mortification battle inside her when she flees Maple Grove. It aggrieves Olivia, to feel like a damsel fleeing distress. But it feels unbearable to stay a moment longer. Disgust swirling thickly in her belly, she rips the jacket off her shoulders. She's already shaking—what did the cold matter? She flings it at the hood of his stupid truck. Bile sits burning, acidic, at the back of her throat. She swallows it down forcefully. Unshed tears may burn her eyes, but there's no way she's letting a single person watch them fall.

She'd woken up feeling bold, and strong, and wanted. Now, with the turn of a table she hadn't spun, she was just a joke. *Who else is he going to tell it to?* She can't think about it. The chunky soles of her boots pound mercilessly against the pavement as she races back to her gram's house. It isn't hers. It is just another counterfeit. And it had been her mistake, to begin feeling like she could belong here after all.

All she has is an empty house.

She doesn't want to go to it—to confront the bed she'd woken up in that morning, serene. *Stupid.* She goes around the house instead; she presses a palm to the sign she'd painstakingly painted, looking at it through blurring vision. She shoves open the door with desperation.

34

The sight of it buckles Liv to her knees.

Ethan

He didn't have to think about it. Ethan shoved the rest of the sheets into Liam's arms, shaking off his guilt. It wouldn't help. Only one thing had a chance—and that was telling Liv the truth. He's gearing up to chase after her when Betty Lou appears out of nowhere, wrenching Ethan backward with a surprising amount of strength.

Somberly, she instructs, "Take your *car,* you silly goose."

When he keeps standing there, baffled, her fingers snap in front of his face. It's an action that reminds him so much of Olivia, it feels like a key put into his ignition. Just like that, Ethan's back in motion. He thinks of her every step of the way.

He thinks of her when his eyes zero in on the jacket she'd left on top of his truck. He thinks of her when he vaults his body over one of the tables, standing in his way like a barricade he has no patience for— thinks of how it had been only weeks ago that she'd snapped at him in a diner, and last night he'd fallen asleep with the smell of her skin clouding his head. He thinks of her when he jams his key in and the truck's engine roars; he thinks of how he doesn't know how to sit in his own driver's seat and not think about her hands on his steering wheel. The way something so little could make someone so strong look so *caught.*

The radio blares automatically, before Ethan silences it with a forbidding twist of the dial. And he thinks about how Liv is the worst singer he's ever met, but how no one has made him laugh this hard since he'd been eighteen and met a friend he wanted for life.

He's certain he breaks at least one speed limit rushing back to her door.

Ethan hasn't prayed since his dad's funeral. It's one more thing he doesn't like to think about, because there's no light there. Racing through Maplewood Grove, he can't help but think a single, piercing word in the direction of the first person who felt like light to him in so many years: *Please.*

Olivia

She isn't sure how much time passes before he walks in. The garage door shrieks in protest when he forces it upwards to admit his considerable height inside. He finds Liv curled up, sat in the middle of wreckage. There's toilet paper hanging in strings around the ceiling pipes. All around her, tools are scattered.

"Jesus, Liv." She watches Ethan's jaw drop. She doesn't know if she should believe him.

Liv lashes like a knife to her own ears when she asks, "Is this part of it, Ethan? Did you do this? Just tell me, please. If I'm gonna feel like this, I might as well know the whole tr—"

"I *came here* to tell you the truth," Ethan says. If she explodes when she's angry, he implodes. She was sure she knew what he looked like when she pressed his buttons. She'd spent considerable time aiming for them these past few months. But, no.

Now she sees it, the way Ethan's anger casts a shadow over his features. The way betrayal weighs on his breaths, his shoulders pulled back like they are recoiling from her. "I would never. I would never disrespect anyone this way, Liv—*especially* not you. If you're not going to believe anything else, at least believe that. What would I even have to gain from this?"

"Destroying my business," she points out matter-of-factly.

Incredulity seeps into his words till they ooze with it. Ethan looks stricken, asking, "Why, Liv? *Why* would I want to do that?" Liv says nothing back. Waits. Until he exhales, exasperated. "You still think my not hiring you had to do with your acumen," he guesses.

Slowly, she nods.

Never in a million years does she expect him to drop to his knees in front of her, taking her face in his hands. She's too shocked to jerk back. He already has her, close enough for the tips of their noses to bump. "Olivia." Ethan looks deep into her eyes. "I need you to listen to me." His breath is warm against her mouth. She summons a glare.

"Good girl," he says, prompting the nails she digs into his forearm. His brows raise, as if to provoke, *So?* "I was kidding with Liam. We all have our things—mine is dry, deflecting humor. Yours is... Making me laugh inopportunely. Usually after the moments I've tortured myself baring my soul to you. Also, flipping out and making my head spin with your point-five-second rebound rate right back to your regularly scheduled sass. You have a lot of things."

She opens her mouth to argue, and Ethan's lips press to hers instead. "My turn," he breathes against her lips. Her eyes are wide, and her heart beats a tattoo against her skin.

"The only thing I said to Liam I meant was that... Well, I do think you're insane." Again, she begins to object. This time, his lips press to her cheek. ""You're insane, and I can't stop thinking about you. I like you so much. I'm on your side. I just didn't have the money to pay you when you wanted the job. I didn't think you'd label me a sexist jerk against female mechanics. *Man*."

"But Betty said—"

"Liv, do I make you feel seen?" Her fingers pinch and tug at the hair on his arms in objection. But her forehead bumps back into his, a quiet confirmation he can translate just fine. Ethan's fingers tug the thick curtain of her hair behind her ears. "I know you're big on equality. So, I'm gonna need a few things in return," he says, tugging on her earlobes. She shoots him another glare, and he dares to beam in return. Something inside of her melts. "First, I need you to see me back. Not some rumor you heard, not your fears, but—me. Who I am. Who you *see*."

There are tears in her eyes again. Ethan sweeps them from her lashes like he'd once wished to do to snowflakes clinging to them. "Okay," Liv says. "What's second?"

His smile is beatific now. "Go to our fair with me. Beat me at stupid games and gloat way too much about it. We'll report whoever was dumb enough to mess with a woman like you. But after that, just let me laugh with you."

Chapter Seven

OLIVIA

The autumn breeze is chillier than it had been all day, but Liv's face is warm. She breathes in deeply, the air perfumed with cinnamon, caramel, and buttery popcorn. Everywhere she looks is blanketed in a patchwork of warm, vibrant color. The sound of laughter, some shrieking and others from full bellies, permeates every molecule that seeps into her pores. Liv understands how those fairy lights strung everywhere must feel—merrily twinkling down on them all.

They only just walk in, and the party is already in full swing. Everything the two of them had planned, firing off ideas back and forth with competitive zeal, it is another thing entirely to see it stand in front of them—for the whole town to admire.

And they do, everywhere. Over here, where Patty Sullivan sat letting people pick characters for her to paint on their faces. Over there, where gaggles of friends sequestered round the bonfire, gossiping over melting marshmallows skewered on their sticks. There wasn't a single glum face in the bunch of them. A significant amount of *Ooh*'s and *Ahh*'s made it to the pair through the brilliant cacophony of the evening.

Olivia's cheeks ache, but she can't stop smiling. It doesn't help in the slightest when, upon spotting them, their esteemed mayor scurries to a podium that somehow always managed to be erected at any town event. She doesn't know what to do with herself—and that's before Mayor Beckett's voice booms, cutting through the chaos, "Everybody! Everybody give it up for Liv Wright and Ethan Parker! Go ahead—*clap, clap!*" He cheers too, applauding raucously himself, jovial and rosy-cheeked with enthusiasm. "Come on up, folks!"

Olivia considers walking backwards until they are obscured. Instead, Ethan's fingers slot between hers and he tugs her through the throng; not leading her, but walking beside her every step of the way. "It'll be fun," he says. She hasn't been on a stage since her graduation ceremony, but she lets herself lean on him.

Even with the music, it isn't possible to miss the whispers that spread amongst the spectators. The looks they are shot, somehow more daunting when a sea of them is aimed *up* towards the stage, vary from curiosity to outright disbelief. Even biting her lip doesn't keep Liv's snort at bay. From the view, she searches for the people who have become a little bit hers. Liv finds them: she catches Loretta's eager thumbs up and Dot's approving grin; Liam's vaguely apologetic applause and Betty Lou's hands making a heart. Noah, curiously, stands at the corner of the marquee beside a red-haired woman in an apron and a smile like sunrise; he can't seem to tear his eyes away from her.

She can't dwell for long, or hold in her amusement anymore. In a moment, Liv giggles at the sight of Mabel and Agnes Carlton bumping one's hip against the other's on a stage. Both of them sing their hearts out, not even bothering to look at the screen displaying lyrics that Ethan had bribed his friend Tyler, a certified tech genius, with free cotton candy to hook up.

Not for a second does Ethan drop her hand—not even when he uses it to tug her body into his side, and drops his head to whisper, right against the shell of her ear, "Want to really make their brains explode and dance?"

"You, me, and my two left feet," Liv confirms.

Ethan

Peeling her bright eyes away from them, Liv crowds close to Ethan's chest. Her head tilts towards the karaoke stall without her attention ever leaving Ethan. Both of her palms press against him when she says, "And you thought *my* singing was a problem?" In coy imitation of him, Liv cocks her brows.

"No, I think your smart mouth and stunning eyes are a problem," Ethan counters, his hands catching on her waistline. "Your singing could be a weapon of national warfare. Much, much worse than old lady karaoke, Liv, I swear."

Liv's laughter joins the syncopated chorus of it all. Her gaze latches to his, tenderness blossoming between them as if it were the depth of spring. "Aren't you s'pposed to be all sweet on me now that we're kissing partners, Ethan Parker?" she drawls.

He may never be a truly spontaneous man. But he remembers to shut her up, and shocks her when he suggests, "What if we were business partners, too, Liv Wright?"

Just maybe, he shocks himself too.

The End

Sweet Treats

Chapter One

NOAH

When he gets out of his car, he's still rubbing sleep out of his eyes. A quick look at his Rolex says it's only eight-thirty. Too early for him to be awake, considering how late it was when he'd driven into town the night before. But in the same way noise bothered the people of Maplewood Grove, it was the *silence* that made Noah Harrison antsy. There had been too much of it these past few weeks. Yet the reason couldn't be begrudged.

His best friend and business partner, Ethan Parker, had gone and fallen head over heels in love. Noah's blanket invitation to sleep in his usual room in Ethan's house hadn't gone anywhere, but Ethan often did. His girlfriend lives across town. These days, wherever Olivia Wright is, Ethan wants to be. Of course, Noah is thrilled for them. It may have been a little over three years since Noah had been in a relationship so committed—but he remembers the dizzying, pulse-tampering high of a honeymoon phase. When you couldn't get enough of each other. It was a *fun* phase.

It was absolutely more fun than being a third wheel in it. Especially when one's *fellow* third wheel—and third member of their trio, Liam

Brooks—had picked sleeping in over breakfast that morning. Fortunately, Noah has other friends, too. Other *close* friends, even.

Because that's what Hannah Baker is to him. His *close* friend.

Surely that eliminates any weirdness from her being the first person he'd wanted to see that morning. It would be reading too much into it to say he'd felt relief flare in his chest when Liam had declined his invitation to grab a bite together. So what if he hadn't had to call Hannah first? It wasn't a bad thing that he knew where she'd be. Or that he knew exactly how she liked her coffee. Friends brought other friends coffees. Sometimes, they also brought along poppyseed bagels with cream cheese and jalapeños. It's the kind of friend Noah was.

He'd bring one to Liam, too, if he'd said yes, he thinks, pushing open the door to Sunrise Bakery. The glass door through which his eyes lock in on Hannah before he's even inside. Noah sips a big mouthful of his Americano.

His eyes actually burn from the lack of blinking. It had to be a side-effect of the sleep deprivation that he couldn't stop staring at her. Not that Hannah doesn't *deserve* to be stared at. She's a pretty girl. With dramatic red hair and soft bangs that frame her deep emerald eyes. Not to mention the precious freckles that dust over her nose and cheeks like cocoa. But none of it is why he can't look away. It's just her energy. Undeniable energy. So present in the soft lines of her face. Present, too, in the way the bakery he'd watched her dream about and build from the ground up bustles with people first thing in the morning—and the noise, the pressure, the *chaos* of it all doesn't diminish her luster one bit. She just glows, like the sun rests beneath her porcelain skin.

"*Noah!*" she chimes the second she catches sight of him. Her voice cuts right through the din. A fist squeezes Noah's heart in his chest. Hannah's smile is as warm as the middle of June. Fall's frost had no choice but to thaw from his weary bones. Who could resist grinning back?

"Look what I brought my favorite baker," he announces, holding up two bags like a prize.

Her jaw drops in genuine delight. She always feels everything with her entire face. It was one of his favorite things about her. "You're a prince among men, mister," Hannah beams, waving him on over with a momentarily free hand.

Noah shrugs a single shoulder. He wanders closer but doesn't slip behind the counter yet. He likes watching Hannah in her element. "I know how much you hate sweet things for breakfast." He nods, partly to himself. *Friends remember things about you.* "Even if that's really weird because you're literally a baker. That's like if the Pope didn't like Rome."

Hannah laughs her full-bodied laugh. Noah's belly warms just hearing it. "I'm not sure if I should be more flattered by being compared to a religious leader or that you just called my little bakery Rome—but thank you." No one blinks twice at their exchange. All the while, Hannah bags orders. One with more croissants than Noah can keep count of. Another order of a scone, throwing in a small container of jewel-red jam alongside. A box she slides a slice of pie into; apple, he smells.

Eventually, the herd dissipates.

She doesn't even look back when she heads behind the counter, knowing he will follow. By rote, he trails after her into the bakery's kitchen. There was only a half-wall between the display case and the kitchen; Hannah liked her eyes on everything at the same time. He watches her set the bag down, her delicate fingers extracting goods from their packaging. The precious, bright beam she gives him for something so small makes Noah feel unsteady. He leans against the wall for support.

"I was grabbing something for myself anyway, not a big deal at all, Han," he says gently.

"It doesn't have to be a big deal to be very, very sweet of you," she returns, clinking her coffee cup against his. "Trade you a muffin? I just made a fresh batch. Blueberry. Your favorite."

See? Friends gave friends treats. "Deal," he says, downing another mouthful of coffee.

"Ethan at Olivia's again?" she asks with a knowing smile.

"You know it," Noah pouts pitifully, fighting a grin. It's a battle he loses almost immediately. "I don't know why they're even pretending they aren't essentially living together. And I get it. Julia's house beats living over the shop. It feels a little sad when Ethan isn't there—"

"—And he's been there alone plenty when you're in the city," Hannah chips in, gesturing to him with her bagel before taking an enormous bite out of it. He'd figured she hadn't eaten yet.

"Right. Besides, with the merger and everything, it makes the most sense," he says.

Hannah nods along, chomping through a few more bites. "So, how're you coping? Have you thought about—?" Noah's already shaking his head. He knows where she's going. As much as she knows why the answer is a resounding *no*. Her gaze softens with sympathy. "Still?"

A single shoulder lifts in a shrug. "Still," Noah confirms. "Pop's still trying to sweet-talk me into joining the family legacy, like Abel isn't right there and actually made for it. I don't get it." Hannah hums along, listening raptly. She holds out the second bagel to him.

There's no pressure, only understanding, when she adds, "Don't you, though? You're their oldest. I'm not saying—" She pauses, sucking cream cheese off her thumb. Too invested in what she's saying to notice how hard he gulps. "—it's fair. It's not. It's messy. But people have expectations, Noah. Parents are people. None of us know what to do when life doesn't follow our plans. It's just that some people have solid plans, like... Look at Grace, you know? Grace has a five-year plan. A ten-year plan. *Probably* a twenty-year plan. She's so productive. And, you— you're the busiest guy I know. But you're not that way. You don't do plans because you love the independence and the..."

Automatically, Noah supplies, "Freedom?" He forgets, for a moment, that it's him she's talking about.

Eagerly, she nods back. "Uh-huh, that. Yes. You find freedom in rolling with the punches. It works for you. Not– Everyone isn't like that. That has to be okay, right? Sometimes, you just have to meet people where they're at."

Noah quiets. It isn't easy when Hannah continues to look at him: eyes wide, curious; her mouth, uncertain, never okay with offending anyone. It's necessary. A moment to shut his eyes, swirling her words in his head, feeling the weight of it all. She knows what she's talking about, is the thing.

His parents and his little brother—his *neighborhood*, actually—aren't a mystery to her. Hannah gets it. She'd had a first-row seat to his childhood (and him, hers) from right next door. She understands the weight of the privilege and the rickety bridge of discomfort when discussing that weight. Some of the closest people in both of their lives would've had wildly different life stories if they'd been dealt the same cards. Hannah's best friend, Grace Thompson, was a self-starter who'd worked multiple jobs while putting herself through college—and was the first in her family to go. Ethan, who'd worked his tail off to get into Columbia University, hadn't had the resources to finish out his degree without the scholarship he'd lost when he left to be by his sick father's side before his passing.

Noah can't dismiss her perspective. He never, ever wants to. "I think," he says, eyes opening to latch onto hers, "you're going to get upgraded from Pope to Yoda."

Her bright, explosive laughter makes his belly flop. The sharp trill of his ringtone may as well be divine intervention. He rushes to answer, nearly spilling the remnants of his coffee all over himself in the process. Even to his ears, he sounds breathless when he answers: "Yeah? Hello?"

HANNAH

Hannah watches him answer the phone and takes the opportunity to polish off the rest of her coffee. *Lots of cream, no sugar.* He always gets it right. His schedule may not be, but Noah Harrison was pretty predictable. At least Hannah thought so—and she knew what the opposite looked like. She'd grown up with a wildly volatile sister and a deeply emotional father. Noah wasn't either of those things. There is nothing throwaway with his emotions. From the moment he starts talking, an eleven is etched between his brows, a darker brown than his straw-blond hair.

He was a man who handed out a lot of rainchecks. She was used to it. If there had been a time it had bugged her, it was long enough ago now that she doesn't remember it. Unfazed, she's already packing up a couple of muffins for him. Still hot and in their baking tray.

She tries not to laugh when he hangs up, a guilty-eyed hangdog look on his face. "It's *okay*," Hannah rushes to assure. Most people mistook Noah's carefree attitude for a lack of care. She knew better. She'd seen the effort he puts into being who he is. Easygoing and buoyant. So willing to be there for anyone he could be there for. He revealed his own anxieties rarely. Hannah had wondered more than once if he had forgotten about them himself.

She tries not to be reeled in by the illusion or take his heart for granted. She was lucky enough to be one of the few he didn't pretend with. It means something to her, to have that trust. "Text me later. And take your muffin." She waves the bag enticingly.

"You're wonderful," he says. The reverence in the words steals her laughter anyway.

That's Noah, she reminds herself. "I know," Hannah agrees. "The Yoda way it is."

His boyish grin dissolves into a deep-set laugh that lingers. She barely had time to process Noah's departure before the bell dings again. Like a tornado, her baby sister surges inside. "*Hannah?! Hannah!*" Phoebe shrieks.

"Gosh, *what?* Fee, quit that– *Ouch!*" Hannah laughs, her palms covering her ears.

Phoebe does not. Hannah suspects she's louder even when she

squeals, jumping up and down, *"I'M ENGAGED! WESLEY PROPOOOOSED!"* She yelps, leaping away from Hannah, when coffee suddenly splashes everywhere—exploding when it falls right out of her hand.

Shock freezes Hannah's limbs. Her feet are soaked, possibly burnt. Her hand is over her mouth, muffling, *"What?"* It doesn't soften the sharpness. Not even towards her sister. Her seventeen-year-old, still-in-high-school, *baby* sister.

Her sister, who looks as befuddled as she sounds, says, "We want to do it next week. During... the Halloween Festival. It's basically free decor, right? But will you do the cake, pretty please?"

Chapter Two

NOAH

This may be a very, very bad idea, Noah thinks. But that's more an acknowledgment of a fact than anything else.

He idles in the doorway of his childhood bedroom and wrestles with the urge to run to his car. It's in the sprawling driveway of his parents' house. Tempting. Fuelled up. Its engine was ready to roar back to New York in record time. The sleek, industrial gloss of the city would be a sharp contrast to Maplewood Grove—but an even sharper one to the house he stood in. Feeling trapped, even if he isn't. He hasn't been in a long time. He forcibly reminds his body of that.

The wooden floor creaks beneath the weight of his footsteps. When he flops backward on the bed, Noah can smell the same detergent Delia, his parents' housekeeper, used his entire childhood. His parents hadn't changed a thing about this room. Noah feels the guilt gnaw inside his chest.

Sometimes, you just have to meet people where they're at. Hannah's words are the closest he's got to an anchor. It still isn't a pleasing realization, that it takes effort to keep himself rooted through the flood of memories that wash over him. That he has to force himself to trudge forward. He can't remember the last time he was in here. Everything—

from the debating trophies and swim team medals to the navy and green tartan-printed bedspread—feels like relics from a life that doesn't resemble the one he's built for himself.

He isn't unaware that he could've been somewhere else right then. If not back in his apartment in the city, then back at Ethan's. At *Liv's*, even, since a sheepish-sounding Ethan had invited him to dinner. An apology he'd known Noah wouldn't accept coloring his words. He could've gone to Hannah's pl—

Nope! Nope, nope, nope, Noah cuts the thought off sharply.

Whatever his abrupt and inescapable magnetism toward his lifelong friend seemed to be, he had to find a way to quash it. There were so few constants in Noah's life. By choice as much as circumstance. Only a few pillars amidst the swiftly changing landscape of his life. Ethan, Liam, his siblings—and Hannah. Not in that order. He didn't know what had flicked this switch in his brain, but he knew the opportunity cost wasn't one he wanted to pay.

Who else could have gotten him to do this? Despite the discomfort he felt all evening, there was no denying the joy permeating every line in his mother's face. Maybe it was worth it. Even if it distressed him to see his little brother Abel's face shutter when their father made unsubtle digs about Noah's seat on the board waiting for him. Hannah had a point. It may not be easy or simple, he reminds himself—but no one owed him either of those things.

His phone buzzes in his pocket. He isn't even paying attention when he digs it out—until he zeroes in on the name next to the notification. It cuts through his reverie.

Hannah Baker had texted: *How was your day?*

It had started well because it had started with her. Then, his friend and client, Tyler Reed, had called him for consultation on a product they'd been working on together to launch. Afterward, moments after Noah had slipped into his car, in some ironic stroke of serendipity, his mother had called with a dinner invitation. She'd been so surprised when he had said yes. She'd been so happy just to see him, Noah hadn't been able to dodge with his typical, 'no, thank you,' when she'd asked if he wanted to stay the night.

How would he put that in a text? Hannah hadn't asked *what* he'd

53

done with his day; she'd asked *how* it had been. Noah isn't sure he knows the answer to that himself. But he remembers that she'd told him to text her before he'd escaped out Sunrise Bakery's back entrance.

So, one set of fingers drumming atop his chest restlessly, the other replies: *I didn't forget.* It's a cop-out, and they both know it. It's with a pinch of rare sass Hannah shoots back: *How your day was?* It gets Noah to laugh. Some of the tension in his shoulders ekes away. *Can I call you?*

A millisecond later, his phone is already buzzing with a FaceTime call invitation.

HANNAH

When Noah's face fills her phone screen, his usually floppy hair is matted. She can tell he is lying flat. In a mostly dark room, if the phone light's reflection totally whiting out his irises was any indication. "You look like an alien," Hannah tells him, rounding the cash register. She scoops her purse off the counter in passing. The keys in her hand jingle with every step.

"Aliens are cool," Noah says solemnly, nodding. The movement unveils the real wishy-washy blue-green of his eyes. Somehow, they look duller than they had when they'd parted.

Thanks to the little window in the corner of her phone screen, she has evidence she's faring no better. Yet the difference was, she knew what was plaguing her. Noah, though... "What—" she starts. Pauses, licking over her lips. She twists the key and locks the bakery behind herself. Then restarts, "Did something happen? You rushed off, but you didn't say where."

Noah winces. She watches concern splay itself all over her exhausted features. Just as plainly as her surprise does when he says, "Sorry about that. Tyler needed input on a—do you know him?" The corners of her mouth quirk. Hannah nods, but can't divulge that Tyler Reed happens to be her best friend and roommate's ex-boyfriend. Grace is too private to want that history aired, especially with how it had ended. She bites back telling him the apology is unnecessary—and succeeds. Noah rewards her with a soft, albeit worn-out, laugh. "Of course you do. It's Willow Creek. Anyway, he hangs out a bunch with Ethan's cousin Alex and he passed on my card. Long story short, we've been working together on a game he's developing."

Hopping onto her cherry red Vespa, she tucks her phone into its basket. She hunches close, pressing her earpods deeper into her ears before slipping her helmet on. The engine rumbles to life, and she talks louder over it. "That's why you look like someone ran you over?"

"Do I look like an alien or do I look like someone ran me over?" Noah teases. He is sitting upright; grinning, now.

"Like an alien someone ran over," Hannah says swiftly. "Are you stalling? You're the one who wanted a call, mister."

Noah's grin dims a fraction. Hannah forces her eyes back on the road in front of her. At the late ol' hour of 9 PM on a Thursday, the town's roads are hardly packed with traffic. The quirky jack-o'-lanterns, plastic spiders suspended on cobwebs she's hoping are fake, and various ghouls lining the streets may have outnumbered the people out and about. But she was a careful girl and wouldn't risk it.

It's a good thing he can't see anything but her mouth. She can't suppress her flinch when he answers, "No. I just took your advice. I'm at my parents.' Unfortunately, the evening was everything I should've known it would be. And I did, I guess. Just grueling. C'est la vie." Hannah doesn't say anything. Tension knots the muscles in her shoulders. Eventually, Noah has to prompt, "Han?" It comes out sounding so uncertain, Hannah's hands tighten around the handles.

"Almost home." The words are more strained than most they've ever exchanged. Despite his faint assent, she knows Noah feels it too.

But the beat she takes is important. It gives her a moment to rationalize—remind herself, that Noah hadn't cast blame. She hadn't given advice so much as an alternative perspective. Noah saw it as advice because they were friends. Because he respected her beliefs and opinions. Hannah could control those. But other people's, and the behavior those shaped, weren't in her hands. Noah knew. She knew that Noah knew it.

She was just feeling a bit raw. Maybe unfairly so—but raw, all the same.

As she comes to a stop in her parking spot, turning off the ignition, she rips off the helmet from her head. With her curls already frizzed and tangled from the hassle of the day, it doesn't matter when her hands shake the long auburn locks out. It's a comforting tic before she grabs her phone and admits, "Phoebe announced she's engaged about a millisecond after you left. So, consider my advice crumpled up and tossed in the trash. Sometimes you *can't* meet people where they're at." Noah's eyes widen with shock his features have trouble processing. Hannah suspects it's pretty close to the look on her own face when her sister squealed the news. Give or take a dash of abject horror.

It bolsters her spirits enough to add, "She wants me to make their wedding cake. She wants... More than three tiers. No rehearsal dinner or anything, no—they want to get married in the Maple Grove on Halloween. Free decorations, an open invitation to the town. Because, *apparently,* that's the epitome of romance." Hannah's palm drags over her face. "I also, somehow, got roped into cooking the desserts for reception. All of this, the day after Dot came into the shop and chose me to bake for the festival."

Noah barely chokes out, "But she's—"

"Seventeen! Yes!" Hannah exclaims. She didn't have to question the panic on his face. His little sister, Emily, was only two years older than Phoebe. Not to mention one of Phoebe's best friends in the world. If Phoebe could do it...

"Phoebe?" Noah questions. Hannah can't even laugh at the way his alarm distorts his pitch. She leans her elbows heavily on the handlebars of her bike, holding her phone with both hands. "Phoebe who had a pet ladybug less than ten years ago?"

Hannah laughs, only for her eyes to burn and a lump to lodge itself in her throat. "I don't know how I'm going to do it all. This *wedding,* the Halloween Festival, the— My people-pleasing tendencies have struck again!"

It disconcerts her, the sharp crook of one of Noah's brows. The way he's looking at her... Like he's trying to look inside her. Sometimes she almost forgets, that he isn't airheaded. He was funny and joyful, but he wouldn't be half as successful as she was if he weren't incredibly smart too. He outright asks, "What was the last one?"

Hannah shakes her head. "Nothing it'll help to talk about, Noah," she says. If it's taking advantage to add, "I'm so stressed just thinking about the sheer amount of stuff I've got to do this *week,* I'm about to break into hives," knowing, in her gut, it'll conquer his attention, then Hannah surrenders to the pinprick of guilt. She tucks her helmet under her arm, propping it on her hip while she walks.

She almost trips when he says, "What if I come and help?"

"Uh, Noah, you—"

"—Aren't as talented as you are, no," Noah interrupts like he's finishing her thought. "I've got to go back into the city tomorrow for a few meetings, but I can be back the day after. I can follow instructions. Mix stuff. Be an extra pair of hands, and ears. Listen to you rant about the things you're too nice a girl to say about your sister..."

Even with her eyes burning with exhaustion and unshed tears she can't explain, somehow, he makes her smile. Maybe just because he still thinks she's a nice girl when she feels like a horrible, unsupportive sister.

Hannah sucks in a deep breath, then exhales. "I'm going to spend tomorrow making a game plan. The day after tomorrow sounds perfect."

Chapter Three

HANNAH

"All right, all right, all *right*! Let's get this show on the road, doll," Noah strides in, arms out. His tenor is as loose as his shoulders.

It's 6:27 AM—and Noah's *early*.

She doesn't even realize she'd been waiting for him to bail until he's already there in her doorway. The jolt of surprise is unmistakable. Hannah doesn't have to look down to know the words on her apron are clouded by flour. Meanwhile, his hair is back to its typical oomph. It pairs well with his periwinkle quarter zip sweater and dark wash jeans. He's already pocketing his watch. The man could pass for a J.Crew model. He should've been out of place in her bakery.

But he isn't.

Before she's even done waving a batter-coated hand in his direction, he's unrolling an apron. One he'd brought on his own, though he knew she had a few to spare around the shop. It deems him **License to Grill** and Hannah can't help it—she snorts right into an uproarious cackle. "You're *ridiculous*," she accuses in between spurts of laughter.

"Wouldn't dream of claiming otherwise," he agrees, nudging into her space. "You can still put me to work though. My phone's powered off. Undivided attention, *check*." His spirits have done a total one-eighty in the 48 hours since they last spoke. Hannah doesn't question it. After all this time, she isn't unfamiliar with Noah's disconcerting bounce-back rate.

It's his declaration, instead, that has her features puckering into a frown. "You know, you don't have to do that, Noah," she insists. "I don't mind you having to—"

Noah is quick to interrupt. "What if *I* mind?"

"Um," Hannah replies eloquently.

"Will you just put me to work, woman?" he quips through his winning grin.

She grapples for a moment, surveying the layout of the kitchen. The stainless-steel island, planted in the middle of the room, is currently cluttered with the fixings of cookies. "I was just trying out this new recipe for pumpkin-spice-latte-flavored cookies. Shaped like jack-o'-lanterns, maybe. Cosy-tasting, spooky-looking, you know?" Sneaking a spatula from the counter behind her, she scoops up a dollop of dough. "Taste test?"

Noah doesn't hesitate before taking it into his mouth. "Mmm..." He moans around the utensil and Hannah beams, only to try it out for herself a moment later, and state, "Needs more cinnamon. And a dash of nutmeg, I think."

He just hands over the jar of cinnamon to her. Hannah sprinkles it liberally into the mixing bowl. Until an inhale is enough to coat her tastebuds with it. She folds the batter vehemently. Smiling to herself, she asks, "Do you know what this reminds me of?"

"What's that?"

She can almost see it, now. Noah, Abel, and Emily Harrison puttering about in the kitchen of her family home. Four-year-old Phoebe stealing fistfuls of chocolate chips. Her mother humming some showtune. Hannah watching, trying to memorize the elegant movements of her mother's hands. "That Halloween we all dressed up as Power Rangers and our parents let us go trick-or-treating into town—and all of us slept in the den afterward, watching movies all night," she recounts. Her voice comes out sounding dazed. She looks at Noah. "Do you remember?"

"We were seventeen." He nods. His grin has softened into something sweeter. "The last Halloween before I left, right?" He doesn't have to add, *For college.* Hannah knows. It had been the last Halloween he'd spent under his parents' roof—and the last one they'd shared with all their siblings.

"Yeah," she agrees. It has him looking at her like an equation he can't solve. That tickles Hannah, just a little. "Are you thinking about that because we were the same age that Phoebe is now?" he prompts.

Hannah halts, her hand stilling over the bowl. "Uh, maybe. A little bit," she allows. Despite her sudden inability to not meet his eyes, though, a dam breaks inside of her. She doesn't think before she's spilling. "I've just thinking a lot about time since the other day. About —About how I'm *thirty*. And I'm doing well. More than a few people thought I was nuts for starting the bakery, but I do okay for myself. I can call myself successful without looking like a fool. Professionally, that is. But—I don't know. I guess I never thought I was stuck behind until Phoebe skipped on in with her big news, and now..."

Noah's shoulder bumps into hers. "Now?" he coaxes gently.

She swallows around the lump in her throat. "Now... I'm just rethinking. About whether I've overlooked finding someone. Maybe I sort of took it for granted? That it'd just happen when it happens, right? Love. A happily ever after. *Something.* But I'm nowhere close."

For a long while, he says nothing at all. Enough time passes, in fact, till Hannah tamps down on her mortification and sneaks a look over at him. He looks like he's wrestling with something. She tries, "You can say anything to me. It's okay. I can take it." He shoots her a smile, but it looks more strained than anything. She sees it in real-time, though: he makes a decision in his head. She watches his shoulders loosen.

"I think—" he turns, his hands catching on the swell of her hips, turning her too, "—that you're a special woman. You're one of the wisest people I've ever known. If you wanted a hoard of suitors, you'd have one. I believe that wholeheartedly." Hannah's head fogs. Through her haze, she wonders if she's breathing. She's known him all her life— and she'd never seen his eyes look so intense. For once, there's no levity to be found in Noah's words. "You're brave. Braver than I've ever been, Hannah. You know what you want and you never back down from going after it. And you do it with such conviction, no one can get away with questioning it. If your gut says you'll know when you know, then... It's worth trusting." The way his hand squeezes on her hip is meant to be reassuring.

Her mouth cottons. "Oh," she manages.

Noah doesn't ask her for any more than that. Instead, he simply nods to himself. Satisfied. He doesn't stutter or fumble at all. He just says, "Good. So, tell me about your game plan."

NOAH

Noah doesn't need to look down at his feet to know he's practically skipping down the street. But it can't be helped. He is buoyant with elation. His fingertips were still warm—with the memory of Hannah's cheek heating beneath his touch, after they'd hugged goodbye and before he'd planted her helmet over her head. The entire evening feels like a dream. It's a contrasting kind of fantastical to the spooky, creepy, quirky decor that Maplewood Grove is already bedecked in. He might as well be floating on a cloud.

All it takes is walking into Loretta's Diner, and Liam Brooks punctures it. "What on earth is going on with your face, dude?" His eyes are wide, his mouth flummoxed. He looks questioningly across the table to Ethan Parker, and Ethan's girlfriend, Liv Wright, tucked beneath his arm. "Something's going on with his face. Right?"

Noah doesn't know whether to laugh or frown. So, he suspects what comes out is somewhere in between the two. "Is that your way of complimenting my rugged handsomeness?" he suggests. An obvious joke, given how he was about as rugged as a baby dolphin.

"Nope," Liam says, matter-of-fact, before slurping milkshake through his straw.

He drops heavily into the seat beside him. In afterthought, he shoots a two-fingered salute of greeting the ruddy-cheeked diner owner's way. Stealing a French fry from the plate in the middle of the table, Noah chuckles warmly. "I'll bite," he quips, already entertained. "What's going on with my face?"

Liam opens his mouth.

But it's Olivia who says, "You basically have heart-eyes. Like an emoji, Noah."

He's quick to tease, "You mean the general expression our boy here wears around you?" He gestures to Ethan, who doesn't look remotely fazed.

"Kind of," Liv gamely agrees. "But Ethan's got a tough shell. He doesn't go around wearing his heart on his sleeve." The implication is that Noah does. He doesn't mind. There are worse criticisms to receive. Her vaguely witchy eyes are incising—but he supposes they're always that way. He doesn't see it coming when she asks: "Out of curiosity...

were you just with your little redhead, Noah?" Her voice comes out too knowing.

"Hannah," he says. Too quickly. He already knows he's dug a ditch for himself.

Deadpan, and facetious in a way that could only be inferred when one knew him, Ethan comments, "Well done, Olivia. I can't remember the last time someone earned a glare from Mr. Sunshine." Liam guffaws, enjoying this too much. Noah swipes his milkshake in punishment. Liam just shrugs.

"Liv, you're off this time. Hannah's been his pal longer than we have," he still says. Of course, it isn't in Noah's defense so much as it is a matter-of-fact explanation. "It's not like that. She's gorgeous, sure. He's just too deep in the friend zone. Right, dude?"

Olivia pelts Liam with fries, her head shaking vehemently, protesting, "That's not a *thing*," with a hand laced through Ethan's, keeping his arm around her no matter how much she moves. Noah sucks down a desperate mouthful of shake. It tastes like the cookies he'd just baked with Hannah.

"What do you mean it's not a thing?" Liam demands. Noah dips three fries in ketchup and chomps down on them. A wary, albeit engrossed, audience.

"I *mean*," Liv retorts sharply, combative as ever, and just as passionate, "that's made-up verbiage. That's saying either, one, that friendship is a lesser relationship than a romantic one—and that's just pathetic. Or, *two*, that there could be a better foundation for a relationship than friendship. Which is just loving hanging out with someone, trusting them with your secrets, and laughing with them. Isn't that something you'd want with someone you're in love with?"

Liam is already arguing before she's through, defending, "*Woah, woah, woah*—you're forgetting one crucial difference, Liv. Friendships last longer. Romance is a shot in the dark, and half the appeal is the mystery and chase of it all."

In a rare turn of events, it's Ethan who makes a sound of dissent. It rumbles deep in his throat. Noah is surprised but thrilled. Ethan seldom partakes in their petty squabbles, more often opting to be an amused spectator. That makes his two cents more valuable. "Yeah?" Noah prompts. Liam and Liv fall silent—though the former steals his milk-shake back, first.

"Noah." Ethan at him squarely. It would be unnerving if they weren't past nearly two decades of friendship. "When you hugged her, did you sniff her hair? If you're still thinking about the smell of her shampoo, you're toast."

Slowly, Noah considers that. Years worth of experience in the bowels of corporate America is to thank for his poker face. He nods, then presses on, "And if I am?"

"—Then figure out whether whatever hangup you have is worth it, man. I know you. You're chill about everything except what matters. But at some point, you've gotta decide what matters *more*. Is it worth the leap?" Noah watches him use his wrap around Liv's shoulders like a hook to reel her in. There's reverence to the way Ethan presses his lips to her temple. It feels like a lifetime ago that the couple had been at each other's throats. He watches Olivia's intense amber eyes soften for Ethan.

He doesn't mean for Hannah's face to flood his mind in all its tech-nicolor glory. But there she is anyway. Undeniable. Vivid, this picture of her. Her lashes casting shadows over jewel eyes, over her flushed cheeks. This face he's known all his life... and, lately, can't seem to help itching to *touch*.

"I need another plate of fries," he mutters to himself.

Chapter Four

NOAH

People make plans and God laughs. Noah had always liked that saying.

He had still gone to bed with a plan. He'd never minded laughing at himself. Tomorrow, he'd tell Hannah. He didn't know precisely what words he'd use. But he liked the sound of it; organic, real, in the moment. From the heart. He would take a leap of faith, take a *risk,* and tell her. *What've you got to lose, Harrison?* he'd thought when he'd laid his head on his pillow. Comforted by his best friend's chainsaw snoring down the hall, he'd fallen into the deepest slumber he'd enjoyed in weeks.

Funny, wasn't it, how the universe worked sometimes? Noah would have said so.

But that's before the trill of a landline pierces through the night. Disoriented, half-asleep still, he barely registers the numbers on the clock: glowing **3:28 AM.** A moment later, Ethan is yelling. Ethan yells for Noah. His deep-set tenor is distorted by panic. Noah leaps from his bed with his heart in his throat.

Through the roaring in his ears, he only catches the words *Hannah* and *fire*. In seconds, he's out the door. Maplewood Grove is a small town. For once, Noah's grateful for that. He races through it in minutes, aimed for Sunrise Bakery. The air is pungent with smoke half a mile away. He's already hacking up a lung before the sign is in his sights.

The bakery no longer resembles the pristine, dreamy confectionary he had left only hours ago. The fire department is already on the scene. His hands are in fists. "*HANNAH?*" Noah screams, frantic eyes searching for vibrant red in a sea of smoke and soot. Even to his own ears, the syllables sound agonized. The display window's glass is shattered. *What happened? How—?* His chest is tight.

"Noah!" her voice fractures the din. And just like that, Hannah's there. He wastes no time before he rushes towards her. His arms wrap around her waist, sweeping her off her feet. His face buries in the hot, damp crook of her neck. "You're okay," he pants into her skin. "You're okay, you're okay, you're okay–" Like a mantra, he repeats it, searing the fact into existence.

"You're not wearing shoes," she says, sounding dazed. She pulls back and her eyes are glassy. He hadn't even noticed. He finds he doesn't even care. He doesn't care what anyone thinks either, about the way he doesn't let her go. Not until Grace finds a chair for her and he has to put her down.

Hannah doesn't know where she could've possibly procured it. She must ask about it aloud, because she registers her best friend shushing her, saying, "Don't worry about it, sweets." Given the circumstances, the words elicit a broken, wounded laugh from her lips. Grace looks immediately remorseful. "Sorry, Han. I meant you have plenty to worry about. Don't worry about *that.*"

Swiping a hand over her face, Hannah shakes her head. "I know what you meant, Gracie." Her hand squeezes around Grace's.

Watching Grace crouched by Hannah's side, where Hannah is sitting and safe, Noah breathes a little easier. He doesn't pretend to be operating on anything but adrenaline and instinct when he leans close, murmuring, "I'm going to find out what caused this, okay?" His knuckles gently brush soot off the curve of Hannah's cheek.

Teeth scraping over a trembling bottom lip, Hannah nods. Hoping her gratitude radiates when words aren't enough, even when she says, "Thank you."

Hours pass, night transitioning to dawn and then past it.

Eventually, the fire department leaves, having ruled faulty wiring as the culprit. The crowd dissipates. When Hannah digs her heels in, not wanting to leave, Noah insists, "We'll fix it. Quickly, I promise. I'll call Liam. He's so good at this stuff, he'll have it done in record time. In the meantime, we can use your kitchen. Or Loretta's—you know she wouldn't care." The words sound believable now. Now that the unmitigated terror is no longer shrouding every syllable that leaves his mouth.

On one side, Grace still holds her hand. From the other, his cheek presses to the top of Hannah's head. Her arms ensnare and grasp onto his bicep like a teddy bear she used to have. He can't really see her nod, but he feels it. "You're exhausted, Han. Please let me take you home?"

For a moment, she's so quiet that Noah's sure she's fallen asleep. Then she sighs, "Okay." She sounds so small, he wants to put her in his pocket. Instead, he settles for pressing his lips to her temple and opening the car door for her.

HANNAH

Even in crisis, Grace had somehow had the brain cells to not only lock up after them, but also remember to grab the keys. Hannah tries to do her part by putting one foot in front of the other. The whole time, she's still aware of Noah's hand on the small of her back, guiding.

She suspects she's still in shock. Justifiably.

Except all she can think about is... Why, when her world had literally gone up in flames, had she called Noah? It's a potentially ungrateful thought. Definitely an inappropriate one when he's essentially helping her best friend and roommate escort her home. On top of being one of her oldest friends himself. Unfortunately, it's also a question she doesn't have an answer to.

Not beyond acknowledging that it hadn't been a conscious decision.

Which went hand-in-hand with acknowledging that, if it had been, he wouldn't have been the smartest choice. He silenced his phone before he slept. He flitted between Maplewood Grove, New York City, and other, more exotic locations constantly. She'd spent all evening with him before they'd parted—to even expect more would've been overreaching. *Stupid*.

But it hadn't been conscious.

The fire department had called her. Grace, still awake and working in their living room, had answered. She'd driven Hannah here. Somewhere amidst the handful of minutes the car ride had taken... She'd dialed Ethan Parker's landline. A number she'd had to dig out of her contacts because she had never called it before. Terrified and falling to pieces, all she had been able to think about was him holding her together. She'd *needed* Noah Harrison.

It wasn't a bad thing to need. To Hannah, it was just an unfamiliar one to her. Not even one she often, if ever, actively thought about. Or, at least she *hadn't* until Phoebe broke the big news about her impending nuptials. Was it good news or not, that she could still feel all sorts of awful things about a supposedly happy occasion even if she was in shock?

She jerks away from the hand waving in her face, accompanying the concerned, *"Earth to Hannaaah?"* Grace chirps forcefully. If she's disturbed by Hannah's dramatic reaction, she doesn't show it. She only bobs her head in her typical, self-assured, Grace Thompson way. "Okay, good. Time to shower, Hannah."

Hannah's gaze slips to Noah. She doesn't mean for it to. It just... does. "Um," she stammers, eyes locking on his. He'd already been looking at her. Like a superhero he kind of looks like with his dark blond hair falling in his face and the thin, clinging fabric of his deep green t-shirt, Noah swoops in, suggesting, "Hey, Grace, why don't you go on ahead? I'll get some food in her. It should help with the shock."

Her brain takes the opportunity to keep looking at him. Watching him. Watching him *handle things,* like he had earlier, with his arms crossed over his broad chest and his chin propped in a hand. His head bent low, listening to the fire chief. His features, so solemn. His eyes anything but light when they cut across the chaos to hone in on her. When her sharp inhale had led to a coughing fit, tears spilling in twin streams down her cheeks, Noah had been in front of her in a heartbeat. So close, his forehead had bumped into hers. His thumbs, so much less callused than her own, brushing over her cheeks. The way that he had looked at her...

Hannah doesn't think anyone has looked at her like that in her whole life.

Chapter Five

HANNAH

"How does it look?" Hannah asks, stepping back from the frame she's just finished adjusting. Within the ornate encasing is a fully blown-up photograph of Phoebe and her fiancé. Hannah doesn't point out that it is a photograph of the couple from their homecoming dance—only a few months ago.

"More flowers, maybe?" Phoebe chirps. Hannah offers a tight smile in agreement.

The bride is always right, Grace had suggested as a mantra earlier that morning. *Like you're working in retail and she's the customer.* Hannah repeats it to herself, practically chanting within her head while she gathers armfuls of luscious roses and whimsical calla lilies in creams, burgundies, and oranges to tuck into the already extravagant wreath. Despite the season-appropriate coloring, it sticks out like a sore thumb amidst the Halloween Festival's backdrop. There are people in costumes all around them. *The bride is always right,* she tells herself. The bride isn't her. The bride is the slip of a girl in a resized version of their mothers' wedding dress, swaying in the arms of a gangly-limbed, broad-shouldered oaf.

It doesn't matter that she wouldn't choose this for Phoebe. It doesn't matter that she's only seventeen, because their parents had given Phoebe's stupid boyfriend *permission* to propose. It doesn't matter that it's the day of the Halloween Festival. Or that she's been cooking in the kitchen of Loretta's Diner the last three days, after hours to not inconvenience her—not to mention, stowing pride she didn't know she had so much of and accepting sympathy help. Or that she's exhausted and attending a Halloween-themed wedding in a black sweater-dress she's topped off with a witch's hat. Frustrated. Confused, angry, *heartbroken...*

And maybe harboring an ill-advised crush on her childhood boy-next-door. Not that she's thought about the last one. She's had no time to. Even with avoiding Noah the way she's been, like a coward.

"You're glaring at your sister again." Grace sidles up beside her. Despite putting aside all of her own work to help Hannah out, she'd somehow also found time to dress up as a truly magnificent Maleficent. She would be infuriating if she wasn't unerringly on Hannah's side. She tries to focus on that—on how she has a better friend than most find in a lifetime—instead of the rest of it. She feels some of the tension leave her. Grace agrees, quipping, "Much better, sweets," passing her cider in a mug shaped like a skull.

Hannah takes a grateful sip. "Have you, uh–" Her lips purse, though she knows there's really no point. Grace is too perceptive. She was just also strategic, and *nice,* and would never embarrass Hannah on purpose.

It's only when she turns a particularly beseeching look her way that Grace acquiesces: "Noah?" Appraising the congregation of townsfolk in the Maple Grove, she relays over the rim of her own skull-mug, "He's with his bro-pack. House of Mirrors." *Previously known as Sip 'n Saw.* It was common for bigger establishments around the parkland to offer use of their premises for town events. Mostly because it was difficult, if not impossible, to say 'no' to Dot Simmons.

"Should I—?" Hannah begins to ask. But she halts, stopping in her tracks when a tall, dark-haired man—dressed up as what she can only guess is a zombie doctor—approaches them. She waits for Grace to be Grace and rescue her, slickly slipping them away from a potentially awkward situation. Instead, she reminds Hannah: "This is Christopher.

He's Wesley's older brother." Her elbow digs into Hannah's side till Hannah notices he's holding his hand out to her.

The eternal curse of being a redhead smites her: color floods her cheeks, and there's no way it isn't painfully obvious. Christopher, at least, is too polite to point it out. He laughs, flashing his perfect teeth, and says, "I've been sent to ask you to dance. Though, if this wedding was less weird, I would've done that on my own. You're a beautiful witch."

Despite herself, Hannah titters in response. Uncertainly, she prompts, "Weird?"

She would've assumed Christopher—given the wealthy family Hannah knew he and his brother hailed from—would've been too pompous to let out the snort he does. She *definitely* would've assumed he would've been someone who would never be so improper as to outright ask: "You mean, weird because they're in kindergarten or because it's a freaking Halloween wedding?" When her jaw drops, he laughs again—but he isn't laughing *at* her, she doesn't think. "So, how about it? Dancing?"

NOAH

With his hands shoved deeply into the pockets of his cape, he surveys the lights Olivia had helped him string up the night before. They'd fashioned a scarecrow out of random junk they'd scavenged out of her horror show of a supply closet—then dressed it up as a witch, which now sat perched atop a freshly-painted sign reading **SUNRISE BAKERY**. A ghost haunts the window; potentially scary, but only if Grim Reapers often touted candy canes.

When Grace had told him, a couple of days ago, that Hannah was avoiding Sunrise Bakery until after the Halloween-Wedding Extravaganza, Noah's brain had begun whirring. He'd thought of how, when he'd left Hannah the other night, he'd taken with him the mental image of her looking forlorn and nauseous. He'd spent hours after he'd come back to Ethan's replaying the way she had almost cried when he'd made her mac 'n cheese—before she'd fallen asleep on her sofa. Even now, his stomach hurt to think about it.

Hannah with the corners of her mouth downturned. Her eyes swollen and reddened.

Noah found that he'd do *anything* to change it. Even bribe his friend to bump a job up over five others vying for his attention. Fortunately, Liam hadn't even let him ask twice. No matter how talented he was at his job, he was an even better friend. He'd only asked, "You're into her, aren't you?" Processed Noah's quiet nod. And began surveying the damage the fire had wrought.

He was, ultimately, very good at his job all the same.

Twenty-four hours, and Liam somehow made the place look brand new. Just walking through it, Noah's pulse thrums erratically. Just thinking about the look on Hannah's face when she sees it. All the more so when he can tell how difficult Phoebe's wedding is for her. A potent jolt of adrenaline courses through his body.

It powers him across the town, surging through his limbs while he makes a beeline towards Maple Grove. Specifically beneath the cover of a crimson marquee, looking like it was made of luxurious velvet, where the Baker-Schuyler reception rages on amidst Halloween revelry.

He may as well have been a balloon, full of hot air.

The sight before him is an unforgiving needle that pierces its way through the center of him: Hannah laughing, yes; but Hannah laughing with her head thrown back, while another man's arm is wrapped around her waistline, bracing her.

"Cute, right?" Noah dully registers Phoebe giggling in his periphery. She looks very pretty in her wide dress, if a little like a child playing dress up. It takes him a stunned beat to even realize she's speaking to him. Thankfully, the question is rhetorical. She answers one he can't bear asking on her own: "That's Chris. He's my *husband*'s brother. Hannah looked miserable but, look, she's all cheered up, now!"

His stomach tries to crawl its way up his throat, watching the way this man watches her.

The same way Noah does, with frank, helpless adoration.

Chapter Six

NOAH

Somehow, he ends up in some corner of the festival. Nursing a drink that is too sweet with suspiciously vague alcohol content. It isn't often Noah Harrison can be found with such a stormy look on his face. But this is how his best friends find him.

Noah watches Ethan and Liam exchange a weighted look. Frankly, they're about as subtle as a pair of zebras in a herd of horses. Noah just doesn't care. Noah—and he'd maintain he is aware as he does it—is *sulking*. Possibly a never-seen-before occurrence. Hopefully not to be a recurring one. But right then, it feels like the gracious choice to make. After all, his capital-G, capital-G Grand Gesture, as his little sister liked to call it, had gone belly-up. Whatever look on her face Hannah Baker would have when she saw that the business that was practically her child was no longer in shambles. He wouldn't take it back. She deserved joy.

It wasn't her fault he's a fool.

"Looks like you were right," he toasts to Liam caustically. It causes the two men eyeing him warily exchange another look. This one, Noah reads as: *Oh boy.* He supposes that is a fair assessment.

Slowly, Liam asks, "About what, man?"

As if he'd only been waiting for the prompt, Noah throws his arm out. In his vigor, his drink splashes out of his plastic cup, patterned with devious-looking pumpkin. "I'm in the friend zone! She's got a date to her sister's wedding." Liam winces. Noah buries his face in his hands. He hates how cautious his uncharacteristic brooding renders Ethan—he can sense it in the gentle hand his friend lays on his shoulder. "Noah, man," he tries. "That's tough. But you know, maybe it's—" He and Liam exchange another look.

This time, Noah groans, "Just say it."

Ethan's blunt nails scratch at his beard. "I've always admired you, man. The way you take life in waves. I've always appreciated that about you and tried to learn it. If it's not meant to be, then maybe it's just not—"

Again, laughter bleeds in from the periphery. This time, it's a richer, drier sound. More weathered than girlish. The culprit proudly steps into the frame before Noah has to pivot. He sees Dot Simmons, though, and immediately braces himself. He may not live in Maplewood Grove full-time, but he didn't have to be to know the fifty-something woman knew everything about everything. Whether he was ready or not, he was about to get some wisdom. He may as well surrender.

"Hey, Dot," his friends greet in a schoolboy chorus.

"Evening, boys. I couldn't help but overhear..." Dot says, but her deep brown eyes skim right over Ethan and Liam to land right on Noah. He's always appreciated Dot. She was a wise, direct kind of woman. He'd always enjoyed discussing town history with her. She told stories like she was born to tell them. This once, though—and maybe it was the stern look on her face that's to blame—but Noah gets the feeling this wouldn't be the fascinating distraction he wants. "Noah, honey. You know that everybody knows you're in love with Hannah Baker, don't you?"

It was an awful moment to sip on his drink. Because it is in the moment Dot says those words—says, "*in love with Hannah Baker*"— that Noah promptly chokes on his drink. Fizzy bubbles drip from his nose as water leaks from his eyes, burning the way his throat does while he coughs and splutters.

Dot is unfazed. She pats his back, of course, yet otherwise carries on. "You don't tell her though. '*Taking life in waves*',"—she aims a look like an arrow at Ethan—"is something there is a time and a place for. What love isn't worth fighting for? Actions matter. Of course. Greatly. But one shouldn't underestimate the importance of saying things." She taps Noah's cheek, as though she hasn't tilted his world on its axis. "After all, it's nobody's responsibility to read your mind, is it?"

Noah gapes at her. There are sounds that leave his mouth, but none of them coherent.

"I think she broke Noah, dude," Liam mutters.

Dot's smile is serene. She advises, "Think about it."

Like he's one of Tyler's robots and she's the voice of command, Noah does. He thinks of the Fall Festival weeks ago, in the beginning of September. He'd come back into town to check on Ethan, who'd been digging a deeper hole with Olivia Wright than he seemed aware of. His assistance had been unnecessary, though. Ethan and Liv had found their way over their hurdles into each other's arms. In front of the entire town, in fact. He hadn't even meant to run into Hannah. He'd just had another argument with his dad. He hadn't been sleeping well.

But Hannah had handed him a bowl of frosting, bribed him into helping her for a slice of cake. She hadn't needed to. She could've done it on her own, just as Noah needed no bribery to help. But she'd just made it fun. Hannah made everything fun. Just like that, Noah couldn't remember the last time he'd laughed so hard. Until his belly ached with it. Even now, the lips twitch. The memory in his pores, and Hannah's cacophonous laughter in his head.

He was a successful man. There wasn't any point in alluding otherwise. He played to his strengths and did well for himself—did well for *others*, mindfully, using his privilege. Still, nothing made him feel as accomplished as making Hannah happy. That was why he brought her treats and called in favors with friends: he just wanted to make her happy.

It hadn't always been this way. Of course, he'd been fond of her. To know Hannah Baker was to love her; she was too kind a person to not. But it hadn't been any deeper than that. Out of the bunch of them— him, his younger brother Abel, and even younger sister Emily, Hannah, and her little sister Phoebe—Noah had been the oldest. First to fly the coop. He'd still been earning summa cum laude at Columbia when

Hannah had opened her bakery. They'd kept up with each other with errant text messages and consistently remembered birthdays.

How had it gotten to the point where his day didn't feel whole till he'd spoken to her?

He finds it doesn't matter.

"I'm in love with Hannah Baker," he echoes. With the words percolating in his mouth, they sear their truth into his tongue. Undeniable.

Dot nods, satisfied. Then steals his drink, gesturing him on.

HANNAH

Hannah had tried to find Noah—to no success. He hadn't been in the House of Mirrors. Or the Haunted House. She'd looked and looked until her feet ached. Until Grace had sighed, looking winded and fatigued from following Hannah from stall to stall. "Go look at your bakery. Don't question it. Just go." Then she'd actually *shooed* Hannah away.

Standing in her bakery, so beautiful the fire felt like a bad dream, she thinks: *I have the best friend in the world.* She walks through her bakery, taking in everything from the fresh paint to the gleaming counters, and she doesn't know how Grace pulled this off. She sniffles over it anyway. The results. The intention behind it. The *love* in the act—of fixing what Hannah loved most when she'd been too overwhelmed to fix it herself.

She doesn't often let herself need help. But it still feels wonderful to be given such a meaningful gift, without ever having to ask. Maybe even more so because of it, Hannah thinks blissfully.

"I wanted to see your face when you saw it," a voice sounds behind her. She yelps, and there is nothing pretty about the sound. In fact, it sounds a lot like a cat who'd just gotten its tail stepped on. Hannah whips around so fast, her head spins. "*Woah–*" Large hands catch on her shoulders—and slip down her arms, tapering till her fingers are curled into his palms. Noah's warm, musky scent envelops her before his concern does.

"Who sneaks up on someone on *Halloween!?*" Hannah gasps, trying to slow her madly racing heart. As if it will help, she shoves her forehead against his chest. His chest is a warm wall, and he holds her up effort-lessly. There is a metaphor there. Hannah is mournful her brain won't function to comprehend it. Can she blame it? It's already playing catch up. "Did you—?" she asks, lip caught between her teeth.

Noah waits. His eyes are more green than blue tonight. They seem to sparkle, even as the two of them stand in the almost-dark. It makes Hannah very aware he's holding both her hands.

"Did you do this?" she forces out the question.

She isn't surprised it comes out sounding so strained. She's surprised she gets it out at all, given the lump the size of a golf-ball lodged in her throat. Noah doesn't help when he nods. His own features puckered with uncertainty. It's a look she hasn't seen on him in a long, long time —never on the confident and ambitious man he's grown up to be.

"I..." he starts, only to stop. Her heart trips over its own feet in her chest. "I've found that I'd do anything to make you happy, Hannah. I've been told it's an admirable trait, that I don't sweat the small stuff. And my life is just full of the small stuff. But you're not one of those things. You're—"

"Noah," bursts out of her. Only, she has nothing to follow it up with. She can't breathe.

His thumbs drag a line across her knuckles. "Hannah, my life is full of small stuff, but the sun may as well not have come out if you haven't smiled that day."

"But, Noah," Hannah grapples. "How? You're- Your life is so big. It's so rich. It's all over the place, and I'm—" expansively, she gestures around herself, her hands still tangled with his, "—Maplewood Grove. This bakery. My small life and my regular longings. I want a home and a husband, too. And you're... We're friends. We've been friends forever, Noah. What if this—this is just momentary? What if I'm just freaking out because my baby sister got married and it's making my biological clock tick very, very loudly in my head? Because if I'm wrong, and this implodes, and—" Sharply, her breath fissures. Her eyes are burning. Hannah thinks she hasn't cried in her life as much as she has this week.

"But I'm not," Noah says strongly. "I know what I feel about you. You're not a town or an age or a feeling—you're a whole person. And you're a person I can't stop thinking about. I called around, and I'm moving more work here."

"But Noah—" Again, she stops short.

"It's okay," Noah cajoles, tender. "You can say anything to me."

Hannah sniffles, the sound wet and gross. Though her voice trembles, she voices, "What if we lose the friendship?"

Ridiculously, Noah grins. That sprawling, beatific grin of his, like he's got boyish mischief tucked between his teeth no matter how many lines time etches into his face. "I've known you thirty years now, Hannah Baker," he says, using their tangled fingers to tip her chin up, making her look at him. "And the only thing that's happened is that, somehow, I only love you more."

"Do you?"

"More and more."

Hannah sucks in a breath. She wills her heart to steady and her eyes to stay on his, no matter the blood rushing to her face, heating it. Her weight is already shifting to the balls of her feet, propping her up, tipping her closer into his chest.

Her lips brush against his and she says, "Then you should probably kiss me."

Chapter Seven

THERE ISN'T anyone in the history of Maplewood Grove that's been kicked out the Haunted House—until Noah Harrison and Hannah Baker go there on their very first date.

As some seasoned chefs believe, there were ingredients in measured doses that went into perfecting a recipe. Agnes and Mabel Carlton, elderly twin sisters who were an institution in their town, thought the same of a good spooky experience. Every year, they took great pride in having components that came together, making it all bone-chillingly delicious... Character and energy. The suspense. The *foreboding*.

Components, they'd discovered, much to their dismay, that could easily be diluted by an influx of intertwined laughter amidst the ghoulish moaning and creepy jump scares. What was maniacal cackling when there was a hand holding yours? Where there was lovestruck giggling and the suspicious quiet of paramours in dark corners? Fright was lost. Frayed nerves given a balm. *There were days for that*—but Halloween wasn't one of them!

Hannah and Noah don't agree.

But they do weave a path through the gleeful chaos of this little town that loves to celebrate, hand in hand for the first time. With them out of the way, children and adults alike shriek inside of the Carlton twins' haunted house. Outside of it, Liam stands rolling his eyes at a short blonde woman, dressed up at Tinkerbell. Beneath the cover of a full moon, they pass by more than one person they know dressed up as a creature of the night. Their bodies press close together without needing any excuse for them to be. They hold each other, because they want to hold each other.

And as one seasoned baker might come to believe soon, what sometimes made for the most magical recipes of all was something unexpected: like a fat pinch of cinnamon, or relentlessly devoted friendship.

The End

Sweet Time

Chapter One

LIAM

The frigid November morning is as unforgiving as his eyes. Currently, they scrutinize the entourage scattered around him. This is important to him—maybe more than any project before this. Not that Liam Brooks says it aloud.

The dark-haired couple he watches step inside. Their tangled fingers untwine when Olivia Wright turns in a slow, appraising circle. The man's features remain a blank slate typical for him, passive and slack. Her wide eyes unmistakably marvel. She wears her feelings baldly, raw and intense. In a rare turn of events, Liam prefers his best friend's girl-friend's way over his. Ethan Parker is about as easy to read as drywall. Liam's patience dwindles quickly.

"Dude, spit it out," Liam bites out through gritted teeth.

Ethan arches a thick, black brow. "Do I even have to?" he asks dryly, his hand sweeping in a vague gesture. "You know you kicked it out of the park, man."

Liv isn't remotely so matter-of-fact. She grins with all her teeth, feral. "Hate to say it, but you're so stinkin' good at this." So early in the morning, her Southern drawl pours in full force. This once, though, Liam lets it go. His arms cross over his chest, and he soaks it all in.

Nine weeks of tireless work. It had been a labor of love, taking the byproducts of two rival businesses and turning them into a single, sleek, and sophisticated entity now co-owned by two of his closest friends. Some people don't like to mix business and pleasure; Liam isn't one of them. The challenge of merging Liv's and Ethan's shops had been unique. This sight is worth it. Every bit of it—from turning the blemished and stained floor into a durable and immaculate concrete wonder to masterminding the layout and repurposing space to factor in workstations, tool storage, a customer working area, and an office for the pair— adds to the redefined atmosphere. It was a glorious new leaf to have turned, and it had been all him.

"It doesn't even look like the same place, man." Alex lets out a slow, low whistle. Not everyone would've invited their cousin to the unveiling of their new auto repair shop, but Alex Carter was Ethan's friend, too— and, by extension, had long since become a part of their ragtag little group of thirty-somethings.

A small, satisfied smirk curves Liam's mouth. "Now, if only the happy couple would agree on a name..." He trails off. He isn't remotely fazed by the glare Olivia shoots him. He'd been hoping it would peek out, in fact. It's the antithesis to the honeyed sweetness of the second couple sneaking kisses in the still-open doorway, seemingly forgetting they were invited to a newly renovated auto shop walkthrough. Liam swallows down the bitter urge to cough loudly, and pointedly, to break them apart—with a mouthful of the thick, rich hot chocolate one-half of the couple had brought along.

'*Good juju hot chocolate,*' Hannah Baker had declared with an emphatic and sage nod, pointing to the thermos her boyfriend and Liam's other best friend, Noah Harrison, carried for her. Unfortunately, it's delicious. Liam and his sweet tooth never stood a chance.

He turns away from Hannah and Noah's entanglement, just in time to catch Ethan tugging Olivia against his chest, his hands tucking into the pockets of her jeans to keep her close. Liam doesn't bemoan it. He's subsequently impressed with his own self-control. Even as his arm slings over Alex's shoulders, muttering into the side of his tawny head, "If you leave me with these four, I will literally never forgive you."

Alex feigns a wince, whispering back, "Sorry, bro. Gotta go shape the bright young minds of tomorrow!" Seeing as he's already snickering, Liam isn't inclined to believe him. Though Alex is quick to reiterate, "You did good, Liam. Really. It looks awesome, with or without a name."

"We got the two of them to agree to flip a coin, actually," Noah finally speaks up from behind them. *Ah, the way that couples talk in 'we's'...* "Well, it was Hannah's idea. But still." His girlfriend is halfway inside his coat, beaming. Liam doesn't know Hannah very well. She'd always just been Noah's childhood neighbor and friend. But she's pretty impossible to dislike. Liam knows this because he's actively been trying to. For now, Alex is easier to scowl at, slipping out of the garage soundlessly. Like he knows what's coming.

"Harrison, this is your business too," Liam snaps. "Maybe at least pretend to look around?" And maybe Alex had a point. The relief of letting his frustration out doesn't last. It dissipates almost immediately, leaving behind the disconcerted concern across Noah's features.

"I don't have to inspect to know it'll be perfect, Liam. No one here doubts that you're fantastic," Noah says earnestly. Liam feels like he just stomped on a golden retriever's tail.

"Sorry," he coughs out into his fist, draining his Styrofoam cup of hot chocolate. "Well, you guys look through it all in your own time. I've, uh—I've got another meeting across town, so I'm gonna head out." It's a lie. A strained, blatant lie. And he doesn't care. His two best friends are too engrossed in their respective significant others to even notice. The bubbly redhead plastered to Noah's side cheerfully bids, "Hope you have a good one!" Noah looks absolutely besotted. Liam makes haste, getting the heck away from Cupid's Island.

Without Alex here, he's the only single one in the room. It had been part of why Liam had talked him into dropping by, though he'd had to do it before racing to the school in time for his 9 AM class.

Now, he'll have to brave the cold for it. The universe laughs at him in the form of snowflakes that begin to descend from the miserable sky. Yanking the lapels of his jacket closed, he thinks darkly: *How could this day get any worse?*

SOPHIE

It's going to be a good day, Sophie Davis decides.

She takes it to be the universe's stamp of approval when a snowflake falls right on the tip of her nose. Upon impact, it melts. Her nose scrunches in delight. Her mother had once told her that if you were looking for a sign, you would find one. *Luck can be made, darling girl.*

In a place like this town, how hard could it be? Maplewood Grove is something out of a postcard. Often, Sophie's imagination gets away from her. But she suspects it isn't off when her mind conjures imagery of quaint architecture blanketed in snow, with a jaunt through town treating the wandering eye to quirky snow people, gleeful children, lovers huddling for warmth, and endless cozy hot beverages to go around. Maybe she would idle around then.

Today, though, she's a woman on a mission. Her footsteps don't meander; they cut a straight, determined path to a stately red brick building with royal blue and bright white trimmings. Her vintage Sadie Oxford shoes *rat-tat-tat* up concrete steps.

Her friend, Cole, already lingers in front of the reception desk, engaged in an involved conversation with the woman behind it. "—just not safe enough." Sophie catches the tail-end of what he's saying to her.

It isn't surprising. He's Cole to her. But to this town, he's Sheriff Colton Rhodes. He takes his job seriously. He's just about bitten Sophie's head off more than once for not investing in a deadbolt for the front door of her cottage. She bites back a giggle at the solemn ferocity of his expression the plump, pale-faced receptionist rears away from.

Maybe typical twenty-eight-year-olds didn't have friends fully twice their age, but what could Sophie say? She likes what she likes. She makes no apologies for it either—or the red polished nail she pokes the sheriff's side with. "Hiya!" she greets, winking over his shoulder when the receptionist shoots her a look of immense relief. Colton whips around in alarm, but his weathered features smooth when he realizes it's only her.

"You're early," he says, glancing down at his watch. He sounds pleased.

"Well, I can't make a bad first impression on the mayor, now, can I?" Sophie teases. "Especially when you're being so lovely and taking time out of your day to make the introduction. I appreciate it so, so much,

Col—" He shoots her a stern look, bushy brows furrowing. She remembers his insistence on only being *Sheriff Rhodes* in front of 'mixed company,' and chokes on a giggle. She can't take it seriously, even if she acquiesces, remedying, "I appreciate it, *Sheriff.*"

Colton accepts the tea with a firm nod. "You're trying to do a good thing, Sophie. I'm happy to do my part." He says it so gravely, that Sophie doesn't know what to do but grin affectionately.

Which isn't to say, of course, that she isn't serious about this. There are graphs, spreadsheets, and a vision board in the bright turquoise binder she holds. She's thought long and hard about the details. She's the farthest thing from unprepared. She drags a hand through her short blonde hair, shaking out any snowflakes still caught in the thin, feathery strands. She doesn't need the mayor to think she's got out-of-control dandruff, does she?

"Miss Davis?" the receptionist practically whispers, shooting Colton a furtive glance.

She fights the urge to correct her—to say, *It's just Sophie, please.* She can't be friends with everyone. It isn't a bad thing for certain situations to maintain formality. It's necessary to maintain professionalism, sometimes. Not every wheel needs to be reinvented. Sophie tries to remember all of this when she steps up, her smile turning shy. "Yes?" she asks.

"Mayor Beckett will see you now!"

Though she'd known it was coming—expected it, and planned for it —her heart still leaps to her throat. Truthfully, she doesn't know what to expect from Mayor Gene Beckett. Colton was as tightlipped as a person could be. He wasn't one to gab and gossip about the nitty-gritty details. She doesn't wish him to be any different than he is. Yet, as he leads the way through the heavy oak doors, Sophie feels a tender ache beneath her breastbone all the same. *Yearning.* For more girlfriends. The kind that exist in the books and TV shows she absorbs, but still hasn't found in her life so far. She's too familiar with it to not recognize it at first sight.

It's nothing she wants, or needs, to think about right now.

The mayor is already standing up—and he's quick to shake Colton's hand. *A super firm, super business-looking one,* Sophie thinks. "This is my friend, Miss Sophie Davis, sir. She's—new to Maplewood Grove.

She's from the city, like me. She's a good girl. She wanted to talk to you about..." He looks behind at her, gesturing her on.

Oh. "Hello, Mayor. Sir. Um..." Sophie grapples, her mind going blank with panic for a moment. She knows it's practicing her pitch so many times it's become over-rehearsed which saves her. On instinct, she blurts, "I love this town. I've only been here a short while, but I've fully fallen in love with it. And any love worth its weight wants good things for you, I think. And I definitely do for Maplewood Grove. This is home now. And I want to help take care of it. I don't mean to cross any boundaries, sir. But I've come to you with a great deal of hope and initiative. This place is extraordinary, but it needs upkeep it isn't getting. It needs more than just Maple Grove. I've got so many ideas about—"

There is no subtlety in the way Colton clears his throat sharply, cutting her off. He stares at her, and Sophie tries to translate it. She just never gets there.

She's distracted by the mayor beaming at her. Slowly, she sinks into a green velvet chair in front of the gigantic executive desk. The desk is more imposing than the mayor's stature. "Settle down, Miss Davis— *Sophie,* Colton said?" She nods dumbly. His expression reminds her a little bit of the Teletubbies. "Don't work yourself up, sweetheart! We're happy to have you in Maplewood Grove! Lay your ideas on me. We just, ah– This town puts a great deal into our events. It drums up extra income for local businesses, and we feed it back into the town where we can. The budget just isn't what it used to be. With the way the economy is going, you know..."

Sophie is quick to agree. "You're—Yes, you're very right. Thank you. I actually have a plan. If you wouldn't mind just looking," she suggests, holding out her folder. Thankfully, her hands don't shake too noticeably.

"Of course, of course," Mayor Beckett chortles. The buttons of his waistcoat strain over a brilliant blue tie with multicolored seahorses on it. She watches him flip through it—quickly, his eyes moving fast. It isn't like she can accuse him of not paying attention. Harmless-looking or not, the man is the *mayor.* "Goll-*lly!*" he exclaims, enunciating. "This is... Well, this is quite the plan, Sophie. Something of this caliber... I don't know how we'd—"

She can't help herself. She launches back in on instinct, spurred by nothing but the moxie in her bones: "I'll raise the funds myself. I can do it. I just need you to sign off on it. And have faith. That's all!" Her words pour with passion. The poor mayor looks as stricken as his poor receptionist had.

Sophie's grin tastes sheepish when she looks at her friend. *Help me,* her eyes scream.

"Well, ah–" Mayor Beckett says, fumbling, "faith is never a bad thing, now, is it?"

Colton steps in. "I've spoken to Sophie already about how she might have trouble getting some of the townsfolk on board. She's aware and prepared for it. I'll vouch for her, sir." He speaks with such surety that Sophie finds her eyes stinging with emotion. As covertly as she can, she blinks the tears away before they gather.

She tries to sponge as much of his faith in her as she can, steadying her breath. "I'm not afraid to shake things up," she reminds herself out-loud. "All I need is one shot."

Chapter Two

SOPHIE

Gratefully, she wraps her cold hands around the hot ceramic mug. "Thank you," Sophie says, watching Colton pay for their breakfast.

She hadn't had the wherewithal to stomach anything in the morning. With the big meeting out of the way, now she's starving. *C'est la vie,* she thinks, pulling out the sheriff's chair. She smiles merrily at the look he shoots her for it. "I can be chivalrous, too," Sophie insists. She isn't bothered by him shaking his head at her, since he takes a seat anyway.

He doesn't even laugh at her struggle to push his chair in. At five feet and four inches, it's a remarkable feat. One that Sophie is happy to attempt. Her gratitude is as palpable as the folder between them, carrying a contract with Mayor Beckett's signature on it. Whether she could've gotten it on her own or not, it matters that she didn't have to. It matters even more because she knows Colton Rhodes to be a discerning, scrupulous man. His vote of confidence is no light thing—and he'd put it in her.

"Aren't you afraid I'm in over my head?" Sophie asks, shoveling a big bite into her mouth to keep her anxiety at bay. It beats its spastic moth's wings in her chest. When it was her own credibility on the line, it was different. Now, any fall has splash back on a man whose reputation is everything to him.

Cole looks at her sternly. "No. And nor should you be," he tells her. "Now, instead of worrying your hair grey, why don't we go through your game plan?" His words aren't any softer than his severe features. But his intentions are tender. Sophie sniffles, moving a juicy strawberry off her plate onto his wordlessly.

"Okay," she agrees. "What first?"

"Well, Sophie, you need to raise the money first. To know how much, you need to get a proper quote from whoever you're going to hire to do it. The—"

"Contractor," Sophie agrees. "I'll use my New York contacts if I have to, but do you know someone in town who—"

"Liam Brooks," he advises before she's even done asking.

Sophie smiles so wide, her cheeks ache with it.

Sophie navigates her powder blue convertible down the street to the electronic instructions that guide her. *Brooks Built, LLC* is her destination now. Restlessly, her fingers drum atop the steering wheel. Maybe that second cup of tea hadn't been the brightest idea. With caffeine coursing through her system, her mind goes double-time. Maybe even *triple*-time—if that's a thing. She isn't sure.

Then again, it isn't as though her being sure of things is a guarantee. Hadn't she been *sure* that she would leave event planning behind? That had been the plan when she'd quit her job with a leading firm in New York City. It was the city that never sleeps. In it, Sophie had been the woman who never slept, too. No matter how well she'd done at her highbrow job with her highbrow colleagues, she'd constantly felt out of place. Her place in this idyllic small town, with a quiet life doing good... She had chosen it. She had chosen it for a whole slew of reasons. She'd made a plan she'd been sure of.

Yet here she is anyway. Scrambling to plan some event to raise the money she needs—the exact amount of which she must go talk to some middle-aged man about. With any luck, he won't be one of the towns-folk Colton had warned her about... who would take offense to a beauti-fication project. Her tummy aches just considering it.

She can't whine and moan, she reminds herself when she parks her car.

Her shoes are almost too loud against the pristine black marble of these stairs. She finds herself holding her breath like it'll stifle the sound of the steps she has to take. *Life throws curveballs at you,* Sophie grouses. *Isn't that part of the beauty of life—the unexpected?*

LIAM

"*You!*" A sharp, half-gasped exclamation slices the air of his office.

His head snaps up so quickly, his nape throbs from the whiplash. Liam senses the alarm his features exude before his eyes land on her. A short, curvy blonde; natural, but with highlights in hair that's some-where between a pixie- and pageboy-cut. A delicate style that contradicts her bold features; her full mouth all the more so, painted a vivid shade of red. There's no way she's from this town. "Hi?" he says, and it comes out a baffled question.

He watches her plant her hands hips that flare from a petite waist-line. She snorts at him. It's a more derisive sound that she looked like she would make. "We've *met*," she practically hisses at him. Just like that, with her nose scrunched up and venom on her tongue, Liam recognizes her. From Halloween, barely two weeks ago.

"Tinkerbell," he greets. He can feel his jaw tense. "What, are you *stalking* me?" From what he remembered of her, he wouldn't put it past her. Nosy, bossy, *odious* woman. Considering even the little he knew about her, it seemed on the nose for her to have interrupted his day like an arrow through the chest. It's how he'd met her the first and only time he had, too. Pounced upon on a random sidewalk outside of a haunted house, all because he'd made a quip about her costume. He didn't even remember what it was, now.

Whatever it had been, though, was enough to have her ears turning red now. It makes no sense for someone so adorable to be such a massive pain in his behind. She looks vaguely constipated, her lips pressing into a thin, hard line. Liam can *hear* her think, she does it so intensely. "Tinkerbell?" he prods.

"My name..." she says through clenched teeth, "...is *Sophie*. Sophie *Davis*."

Liam doesn't plan it, but still returns, "Tinkerbell suits you, though." Her cheeks suffuse with color. 'Sophie' suits her too. He doesn't know what it is about her. She makes it too much fun to press her buttons. Especially when he can *see* her actually, *literally* bite her tongue. It isn't hard to discern she needs something. "What do you want?" Her nostrils flare comically with her exhale in response. If she were a dragon, Liam ventures she'd be breathing fire. It's entertaining as hell.

"I'm guessing that's what you're here about?" He points to an ostentatiously turquoise folder tucked under her arm mostly to shock her. It works. Her dark brows shoot halfway up her wide forehead in one go. Liam almost starts laughing, watching her force her feet towards him.

"Don't relish this too much," Sophie says, nearly throwing it at him. It sounds like a threat. Despite his day so far, that elicits a grin. It's hilarious watching her falter. She doesn't wait for him to invite her to sit before she drops heavily into one of the pair of chairs in front of his desk.

Usually, he'd have too much respect for a prospective client to do this—for her, though, he kicks up his feet on top of the desk, just to irritate her, before he starts thumbing through her folder. It's more in-depth than he thought it would be. Someone like her, with a punk haircut to go with her leather-and-silk outfit, gave off an incontrovertible vibe; it just did not scream *Type A*. That was probably him with his navy button-down and gray chinos. "I'm interested," he says bluntly. With nearly all of his friends otherwise occupied with their heads in the clouds, it isn't like he doesn't have the time to spare.

"You— What?" Sophie blurts, eyes bugging out. Her mouth gaping like a blowfish, opening and closing and repeating.

Liam doesn't explain himself any further. He simply says, "Just the community garden will run you about $20,000. Obviously, the crew's wages are included in that. Do you want a separate budget for the rest? If you tell me more specifically where you want to start and where you are with the permits, I can—"

The blonde makes a wet, choked sound. Liam wonders if he should be concerned. Any other emotion has to battle his amusement, but it could win the fight if she gets any redder in the face. Her knuckles are blanched with how hard she holds onto the arms of the chair. It takes her a couple of more strained breaths to blurt out, "I— The community garden. Let's just start with that. That's— I have the permit for that. I have to deal with the rest at the next town meeting."

Liam gives her a swift nod of assent. "That's fine. Do you want to discuss the process, or just give me a cheque and leave your folder?"

"I— Uh..." Sophie's nails scratch at the leather arms of his chair. Liam nearly tells her to knock it off until he makes himself relent. Frankly, she looks like she's about to combust.

"What's *wrong* with you?" he asks. It comes out sounding harsher than he means for it to. He knows it even before he sees her flinch. Immediately, he starts to apologize. He supposes he shouldn't be surprised that she doesn't let him get through it.

Instead, she sighs. "I have to raise the money first. The town... doesn't have the budget. I needed a quote from you, to know how much I have to raise. This was a preliminary step." She smiles at him, but it's more of a strained, tight grimace.

Liam can't help it any longer. He *bursts* into laughter. "Right, well, good luck with that!" The only thing the people in this town hated more than minding their business was shelling out money they didn't have to. If he didn't know she was new before, he knows it now.

"What's wrong with *you?*" Sophie spits, at once fragile and biting. *Like shattered glass,* Liam thinks unbidden. The kind he used to make mosaics out of back when he had more artistic pursuits. "Col— *Sheriff Rhodes* sent me here. He recommended you because he said you're not just good at your job, but a good person, too. He isn't usually wrong. But I guess everyone has off days, huh?"

It's his mouth that's forming into a hard line now. "Many things,

Sophie," he answers, matter-of-fact. "Regardless, I'm happy to help. I didn't turn you down, remember? This is a cool project. And Sheriff Rhodes isn't entirely wrong. I *am* good at my job." He hates that he hates the way she's looking at him now: more disappointment than firework-wrath. It cuts him.

"Come back when you can afford me, and I'll see what I can do."

Chapter Three

LIAM

At 4:07 PM the next day, Liam's phone buzzes with an ominous text message: *meet me here!!* He doesn't know anyone who would send him two exclamation points. A second later, a pin location follows. Only then does the anonymous texter remember to add:

this is Sophie Davis btw!

Liam truly doesn't know whether to laugh—or block her. But he can't block her. What on earth is he meant to say to this? He replies:

You're going to axe murder me, aren't you?

He doesn't specify that he imagines the aforementioned axe to be bedazzled. It seems beside the point.

It helps nothing that she texts back:

thats not how i would choose to kill someone :(

The corners of his mouth twitch, threatening to rise. He grabs his keys before they betray him.

Are you allergic to proper grammar, Tinkerbell?

His lips succumb when she shoots back, *just you.* Then adds:

but i already took my Zyrtec so just come!!

She's witty. He can't deny her that. Nor, apparently, his presence. A fact he's already regretting when he pulls up to what looks... First of all, like the perfect place to kill someone, and secondly, like an animal shelter—if the ratty banner of a flea ridden kitten on it is anything to go by. Liam wonders whether he should have brought some sort of weapon.

Beautiful women, he's learned by now, were among the most dangerous things he has encountered.

Before he gets out of the car, he calls her. The call barely hums on for two rings before her voice is pouring down the line. "Liam?" The way she says his name makes it sound fuller than it is. Potentially, he is losing his mind.

"Obviously," he answers brusquely. "I'm outside. I'm assuming you needed a ride?" There isn't one single other reason he can think of, for her to have called him here. Of course, he wouldn't refuse any woman a ride if they needed one, no matter how much this specific woman irks him. A fact she proves when she outright giggles at him, sassing, "Well, you know what they say about people who assume things... Just come inside." It's almost as an afterthought that she deigns to add, "*Please?*" Frustratingly, she does it in a soft, sweet little voice.

Maybe he'll block her after all. Maybe change his number, after.

Then he gets out of his car.

All he can do is stare at her in disbelief. "You can't be serious."

Sophie rolls her eyes at him, but it doesn't look nearly as caustic as it should. "You know," she tells him, brushing through the thick coat of a dog that is more than half her size, "you're an extraordinarily grumpy man."

Liam scowls darkly. "A grumpy man you unceremoniously summoned," he bites back. He can use just as many syllables, as he shows her. And he isn't using them in an apron with a *paw* on it. "Why, exactly? There's no way you've raised that money already. It's barely been twenty-four hours."

"I haven't," Sophie confirms cheerfully. She lowers her head to bump her nose against the dog's before proceeding to coo at it. Liam fears he's stuck at the pound with an actual Disney princess. He wonders if she'll sic the mutt on him if he tries to make a break for it now. "Look, I think we can agree we started off on the wrong foot. I'm *going* to make this project happen. We're going to be working together, for a long while. *So,* showing you that I'm pretty awesome felt like a good place to start."

Liam can only blink at her.

"What?" she asks, scooping the dog off the stainless-steel table and putting him on the ground. Her cheeks are flushed with the effort. Her blouse beneath the apron is red and white like a candy cane, enhancing it.

"You conned me," Liam says curtly.

Sophie shrugs—but he doesn't miss the sheepish wince he elicits before she ducks her head. There isn't much force to it when she insists, "There was no other choice." With a leg planted on either side of the dog, she ushers him towards the cages. She doesn't look back to see if he's following. It's a moot point, that he does. "Would you have come if I just told you we should hang out?"

Liam is quiet. Until she turns her eyes on him, as much sage as they are warm brown, and he can't keep himself from admitting, "No." He clears his throat pointedly. "But that's because I like the people I hang out with to not have threatened to '*kick my stupid shins*' upon first meeting. And to like me. Which isn't so novel of me."

Her entire face lights up when she laughs. It was like there was a light inside of her, and someone had flicked the switch. Liam is so glad she turns to unlock a pen in the middle of it. "To be fair," she reasons, "you were making fun of my costume."

An involuntary scoff escapes him. "Because I complimented it?"

He hears her sharp inhale more than he sees it. "Because you were *condescending.*" Sophie whips around, eyes narrowed and glinting. "Liam, you said, 'Wow, those wings must've taken you all night—and all for something so pointless.' Then you asked me what I even did for a living. That's *rude.*"

So many regrets. He has *so* many regrets for reaching for his phone. "I didn't mean to be," he finally says. Exhaustion drips from every syllable. He's learned from too much experience that, when someone made up their mind about you, there was no point in changing it. He had long since vowed never to defend himself again. The people who wanted to know him just did. Sophie just continues to look at him.

"Well..." Eventually, realizing he won't say more, she prompts. "Then what did you mean?" His skin prickles with awkwardness. He can't pinpoint what it is about her that effortlessly puts him on the spot. In ways he didn't even know he could be put on the spot! But he doesn't know how she knows to turn away, either—checking on the other animals, and giving him space he isn't sure he would've given her, had the roles been reversed.

It isn't easy for Liam to confess, "Exactly what I said. They were intricate and sparkly. We only have one tailor in Maplewood Grove, Sophie, and he'd prefer to light his hair on fire than make a 'costume'. I knew you made those wings yourself. I do think Halloween is pointless. To have a whole festival for it when there was *just* a Fall Festival is nuts. I was curious about what you did. So, I asked." He braves his way through it. It is all the harder for the way each fresh word makes her bottom lip protrude more and more. He didn't think he would ever see someone *puppy-dog pout* at him in real life.

"It didn't come off that way," she says softly. She looks at him with such open-faced tenderness, that it takes conscious effort for Liam not to recoil.

SOPHIE

Only yesterday, he'd been smug and cocksure. How could the same person look so boyish and uncomfortable a day later? Sophie doesn't know. But she feels certain she's more comfortable not knowing everything than Liam Brooks is. From the moment she'd met him, she had thought it would take baring her teeth to get him to respect her. She was tiny, but she was *scrappy*.

Yet it's tenderness, Sophie is beginning to suspect, that Liam squirms in the face of. There's no implication of why that doesn't make her tummy ache.

Fortunately, they're in the best place one could be, in her opinion. She may have a lot to learn about winning over town traditionalists. She may have even more to learn about efficiently intersecting her event planning skills with an aspiring philanthropy career. But she knows how to make people happy. It's the one thing she's been good at all her life. She doesn't doubt she can do it here, even for someone like Liam, whose frown might as well be tattooed onto his handsome face.

Without a second thought, she grabs his hand. "You live alone. Your friends are all in relationships. Yes, I asked around about you. There's a *very* chatty gal in the post office," Sophie chatters exuberantly, tugging him along. "I think you need a new buddy, and I know who's *perfect*." It isn't like she doesn't feel him stiffen. The hallway is too narrow for their bodies not to collide when she pulls him down the row of kennels. She expected nothing less.

She doesn't take it personally when he stiffly questions, "What, are you volunteering?"

Sophie laughs colorfully. "No," she assures. Liam almost slips his hand out of her hold, till she squeezes it. "I'll let you ask me for that one when you've realized it on your own. I *mean*—" She gives him a sharp tug, pulling him to crouch where she does; not unaware that she wouldn't be able to do so if his considerable stature didn't allow for it. "This little fella. See?" Inside the hutch she unlocks is a puppy. He's milky white, except for his floppy right ear, the area around a beady eye, and a spot on his belly, all the color of chocolate. Sophie's voice drops to a gentle murmur: "He doesn't even have a name."

Whether it's a purposeful choice or not, Sophie doesn't know; she just hears his voice pitch itself low, too—even when he's arguing, "I don't know how to take care of other living things," sounding stricken. "I can't even keep a *cactus* alive." This doesn't stop him from reaching into the pen, his fingers trembling... until they stroke over the puppy's head. *Delicate.* The way hands only ever do when dealing with something precious.

"I'll help," Sophie is quick to say. He didn't say *no.* He could have, but he didn't. "I'll take you shopping for supplies. I used to foster all the time, back in the city."

"Of course you did," Liam mutters unsubtly.

Sophie doesn't care how old she looks, sticking her tongue out at him. She knows it's a smile playing with his fickle mouth when he turns away. "I'm going to ignore that. Because you're *melting* right now. And that can't be good for your reputation."

Liam makes a sound at the back of his throat. She doesn't know whether to interpret it as thoughtful or dismissing. He doesn't let her wonder long. He tells her, "I don't know the first thing about taking care of a dog, Sophie." He sounds so sad.

"This is part of why I called you here, you know," she admits. "I've been volunteering here all month. I've been around animals most of my life, really—I was an only child, growing up. My mom had me pretty late. So, we had a lot of animals. Dogs, cats, even a duck; like in *Friends*, you know? And I know that people can be bad judges of character sometimes. We all have blind spots. We all can't help our darn egos... But animals can tell. If he trusts you," her chin juts out, aiming at the puppy now happily drooping his head into Liam's palm, "then it's because you deserve it."

She watches Liam scratch the puppy's floppy little ear. "A name's important. I don't want to pick one on the spot." He doesn't say it outright, but he says enough.

———

She doesn't know what she's expecting. It just isn't what she walks into.

She'd paid no thought at all, to what Liam Brooks' house looked like. The pretty girl who worked at the only post office in town, Betty Lou, had called him *'dreamy'* and *'the town's most eligible bachelor'* ... alongside a long string of adjectives that Sophie had a hard time not laughing about. A bachelor pad, she supposes, is what she'd expected. However one defined one of those. Something with a foosball table and vinyl leather recliners, Sophie imagined.

Liam's sprawling penthouse doesn't look anything like that. It's spare and clean, despite the considerable square footage; dark wood floors, cool-toned walls, and eclectic, moody art. Nothing one would expect to find in an apartment in Maplewood Grove. "*Wow*," she can't help but exhale. He doesn't give her time to feel self-conscious about it, quick to quip sardonically, "Thanks. Now get to puppy-proofing this place, princess."

Sophie giggles, tossing a rainbow-colored rubber ball right at Liam's head. Puppy chases after it, yapping happily, tail wagging with determined ferocity. "*Rude,*" she declares. But she's no longer on the qui vive about it.

"I'll make you dinner while you do it," he adds.

She thinks she may not be as comfortable with not knowing everything as she'd thought.

Chapter Four

SOPHIE

All sorts of things could distort someone's impression of you. A person could fight against that. Try to change it. It would be an admirable cause to fight for; a worthwhile hill to die on. But today, Sophie's scaling another one.

She'd put a lot of thought into her ensemble. She wanted to look nice, yes, always—but this was more than that. Stood in front of her reflection, she'd asked: *Who do I want them to see? Who do I want to show up as? What do I want this to say?* Big questions. Weighty ones.

Ones with answers: This pair of distressed jeans with wide, frayed-edge hems, all country chic. A tie-dyed t-shirt in blues and purples with line art of a woman dancing, her head thrown back, and her mouth open as if in a scream. A reminder for herself. An oversized blazer in stark, bright white; non-threatening. With massive gold, vintage buttons skirting the lapels, that she'd sewn on herself. *Who didn't take someone in a blazer seriously?* Electric blue heels to top it all off, because she's lightning in a bottle.

Anything can be a sign if you're looking for one, her mom had told her. So, she'd decided to become one for this evening. She wants to be a signal they see, like a lighthouse. She wants to be able to tell Colton he's being ridiculous for the nerves he wears plainly for her to see, after. There's a podium for her to walk up to, beside which Mayor Beckett nods encouragingly.

It starts smoothly enough. She clears her throat and opens up her folder. Tucked right at the beginning is her pitch. *Doesn't it bode well, that she doesn't have to look down at it?* She knows it by heart. "Hi everybody," she greets, bolstered by the number of faces she sees smiling back at her. "Some of you know me, some of you don't yet... But it's my hope you will soon. I'm Sophie. Sophie Dorothy Davis, but you really don't have to full name me, ever. That's something my mom does when I'm in some serious trouble. All I want is the opposite here. Please believe that.

"When I came to Maplewood Grove only a couple of months ago, I fell in love with it completely. Quickly, it's become home. From you wonderful people who fill it, and the places you bring to life. But, I—" The moment she says it, she can *feel* the palpable, pregnant silence that saturates the room. She tries not to stammer. "I only want good things for Maplewood Grove. There's so much potential for growth here. It could be so much more thriving. There are gaps that need to be filled, for example—"

"*Excuse me.*" A rich, intelligent voice cuts her off. It's a woman. Sophie knows her. Anyone who lived in Maplewood Grove did: Dot Simmons was a local legend. The fifty-something woman was the unofficial town-historian. She knew everything about everyone. Her first name was the same as Sophie's middle one. She didn't need to know much more to know that, if Dot didn't like you, you were pretty much toast. Dot doesn't look like she likes her at all. "What makes you an authority on the matter, Sophie?"

A scattered chorus of agreement rings out. Dot doesn't pause for their applause any more than she does to keep watching Sophie grapple. She barrels on: "I'm sure you're a nice girl. But we've had people come through here before. You're from the city. There have been *plenty* of people from the city. This town is absolutely beautiful. There is still room on the streets to breathe. What you want to do is called *gentrification*, and if you think—"

"Let her *finish*, at least, for the love of God," someone interrupts *Dot* now. Sophie is grateful for it because it gives her the abysmal moment to swipe away at pathetic tears that threaten to stream down her burning cheeks. She doesn't even process who it is until he's shot up to his feet. Liam Brooks glares a vicious, stormy glare—and it isn't aimed at her.

Somewhere amidst Dot Simmons' spiel, Sophie had recoiled away from the microphone. It had been far enough away that it doesn't catch, now, the way she breathes a quiet, startled, "Oh."

"Liam Brooks," Dot says coolly. The calm look on her face is enough to make Sophie want to wither away. Liam looks utterly unfazed.

"Dot, you know your stuff. But you're better than bullying someone into shutting up. At least listen to her. I have. She's not trying to make a quick buck off anyone in town. She's trying to help local businesses and provide locals with new opportunities." It takes him speaking up, so eloquently summarizing her intentions, for her to realize she hadn't thought he'd paid much attention to her pitch at all.

"How?" Dot asks Liam instead of her. Sophie doesn't mind. Her vision is beginning to clear again, the tears blurring it dissipating with the spotlight off of her. If everyone in the bar saw her burst into tears at the podium, like the overwhelmed little girl she feels like, she would have to move.

"The start of it is a community garden. We have Maple Grove, but that's official town parkland. It's for our town events and recreational activities. A proper community garden would be for—" Liam waves at her then, shooting her a sharp look she interprets as, *Wanna take over maybe, Tinkerbell? It's your show!*

Sophie nods to him. Picking up right where he's left off, she keeps her eyes on him when she finishes, "Cultivation. Gardening. Local produce we can not only circulate but also export to towns in the surrounding area. Everything from vegetables and fruits to flowers. And that would just be the beginning. A percentage of profits would go into the upkeep of the town, too. Buildings that are historic—that should be taken care of as such. That bridge that's basically rotting at the bottom. Countless other things."

Now, when she meets Dot's eyes, she doesn't squirm. "And how are you going to pay for all of it, Sophie? I know Gene doesn't have the budget for this. It's a nice thought, of course. But—"

Again, Liam cuts across her. This time, Dot wears her annoyance. Undeterred, Liam's spouts, "I'm helping her with a charity drive to start things off."

Sophie has to grip the edges of the podium to keep from falling off the stage.

LIAM

In the line of seats beside him, all of his friends are sat. Noah and Hannah, Hannah's best friend Grace Thompson, Ethan and Liv, and Alex all fill out a row he sits at the end of. A single look is all it takes to confirm what he already knew: each and every face wears varying degrees of unadulterated shock.

Liam doesn't need to question why. He's shocked, too. Because he doesn't get into town business. It isn't so much a rule of thumb as it is the status quo. The closest he comes to being involved is communal mockery. That's all. Until today, apparently—and, even today, he hadn't intended to say a word.

Then he had seen Sophie's face, the moment the room got quiet.

He'd made her upset before, but he'd never seen her look like this. He hadn't liked it at all. And something in him went rogue. Off-script and off-kilter. Running his mouth—ironically, in defense of the very woman he'd spent the better part of last night grumbling to his friends about on a three-way phone call. *Unbelievable* Sophie Davis, who'd conned him into taking in a dog he was in no way equipped to take care of. (Train? Raise?) Peppy, nosy, *bossy* Sophie Davis... Who was smart enough to know better than to be so *soft*, who was frustrating because she was going to get hurt being like this and she didn't seem to care about it one bit. Sophie... Whose lipstick knows the perfect way to smudge. Who doesn't like him, but has decided she is going to befriend him anyway.

What can he say about it? Liam just shrugs at his friends. Drops back into his seat with a beleaguered grunt, and proceeds to bury his face in his hands for the rest of the town meeting.

When the town meeting finally dwindles to an end, Liam invites himself over. With a frankness he attributes wholly to the precedent Sophie's set, he shows up at her house. Well, her *cottage*. Located right at the edge of town.

His knuckles rap a staccato rhythm on her door till she opens it. Already, she's somehow managed to change her outfit. Gone is the blazer and jeans combo—replaced by something else concealed by the same giant maroon cardigan that swallows her frame. She looks tinier than usual. Just looking at her makes Liam feel spastic. "I brought you good juju hot chocolate," he proclaims to her extremely, understandably, bewildered face.

"What— You—*Juju?*"

"Colloquial verbiage. I'm pretty sure it's appropriation. My friend's girlfriend said it," he explains, forehead creasing as he does. "Can I come in?" Sophie doesn't say anything when she simply steps back. It gives Liam just enough room to come inside, slipping by her. Noticing her knee socks, that have furry little poms on the sides.

When she does speak, she asks, "Which friend?"

"Noah," Liam answers quickly, eager to keep her talking. "Noah Harrison. He decided he's fallen in love with his childhood neighbor a little while ago. Hannah Baker the baker. She owns Sunrise Bakery?"

Sophie shoots him a weak smile. "I know Hannah. She's a sweetheart."

"I've heard," Liam says dryly. He means nothing by it. Still, it causes Sophie to frown.

He's buttressing himself up to understand her when she asks, "Why are you here, Liam? Why—? Why any of it tonight?" She sounds lost and confused. Somehow very old and terribly young all at the same time.

"Because you decided we're better off being friends than foes, remember? And I didn't say anything that isn't true," Liam asserts.

It is the longest minute of his life, the one it takes her to shut the door behind him and lead him through the foyer of the cottage. "I ordered a pizza. It's on its way. Will you pour that for me?" She nudges the arm holding the thermos. He manages a hum of acquiescence, though he's half distracted by her space. He'd call it an occupational hazard if he could get away with it. Interior design may not be his professional domain—but he can appreciate style. Sophie's is so singular. An eclectic swirl of colors and textures that make him sure she put every room in this place together herself.

If there's anything he's taken aback by, it's the messiness. She looks so put together in her edgy little outfits, that it surprises him that she's a little bit of a slob. For some reason, it makes him smile. Which is enough to rouse Sophie's suspicion. "What?" she prompts.

"I like your home," he answers plainly, sincerely. He's almost bothered by how shocked she is by such a simple compliment. He hasn't been that much of a jerk, has he? It's something to ponder as he strides into her kitchen, hunting down a cup for her to pour the thick, creamy hot chocolate into. It smells heavenly. Just the decadently sweet smell of it makes his stomach rumble ravenously. There's no choice in carrying two mugs back to the sofa where she waits.

"Thank you," Sophie murmurs. "Did you really mean it, wanting to help with a charity drive? I'll let you off the hook if you just did it to get the heat off of me. That was still nice of you."

He scoffs, his head shaking at her before she's even done talking. "What kind of man would I be, if I said things just to say them? That isn't who I am, Sophie. I meant it. And I can tell you've got ideas. So, tell me."

She wouldn't be Sophie if she didn't hesitate, Liam thinks. He gives her a moment for it. Maybe even a moment and a half before he knocks his mug into hers for her attention. It works. She tells him: "I've got a *few* possible ideas. Since you know these people better, maybe you can pick? Getting ideas isn't hard for me. I badly need a sounding board, though—and, as much as I love Colton, it isn't his domain."

"Tell me," Liam repeats.

Sophie goes off, rambling, "I was thinking a picnic sort of thing, first. Maybe everyone could bring their own baskets, there could be bidding on them like that one episode on Gilmore Girls—I don't know. And then I thought: Garden party. Since this is for a *community garden,* it would make sense, wouldn't it?"

Liam raises his mug to her, offering, "Makes me think of Alice in Wonderland."

Sophie beams a brilliant grin at that. "Alice in *Winter* Wonderland," she declares, and turns around a sketch he hadn't noticed. It's etched with a charcoal pencil into the back of a napkin. She must've dropped it on the couch when he'd knocked on her door. It's the tea party scene from the cartoon movie—with snowflakes falling from some sky out of the picture's view.

"Great minds," Liam chuckles. Her resounding cachinnation leeches the weight from his chest—one paroxysm of laughter at a time. "Who knew?"

Chapter Five

LIAM

Hot chocolate, as far as Liam Brooks knows, isn't an aphrodisiac.

It's left little explanation for the way he'd left Sophie Davis' cottage the night before. To think, leaving hadn't even been enough. The memory haunts him like his shadow. As it had all night already. The way Sophie had thrown her arms around his neck at the end of the night. The soft '*Thank you, Liam*' she'd whispered into the side of his neck, making his pulse stutter.

How he'd almost kissed her before he'd made a run for it. Like a total coward.

Liam feels terrible, not because he'd gone to her place with any ill intent—she'd been vulnerable, and he wasn't trying to take advantage—but because he hates seeing her sad. The way her face fell had stayed with him all night. Pissed off is fine, when it paints her skin with color that makes her look so very, very alive. But not dejected and drooped, like a decaying sunflower.

If his friends have questions about what occupies him... Well, it's a good thing Liam's got a checklist a mile long to keep them too busy to ask— "What's going on with you and Little Miss Sunshine?" Ethan smashes his thoughts to smithereens. He doesn't employ his own moniker for Sophie; it had been Liam who'd called her that when he'd first met her. It hadn't been in a positive light by any stretch of the imagination.

Now, Liam can't protest. His best friend asks while draping tinsel around a tree.

He's helping for free, just like the rest of them are. All because he'd asked them to. Sometimes, Liam really gets how blessed a man has to be, to be able to take friends like his for granted. Even if they are slimes who needle him with, "Guess all your whining about our finding our girls bit your behind. They call that karma, don't they?" Everything Ethan says is in a dry, deadpan tone most wouldn't know what to do with.

Liam replies with a rude hand gesture.

Alex feigns a wince, managing while he and Ethan carry another humongous table between them for what's slated to be a garden party to end garden parties. "Defensive, man," Alex chides.

His tongue pressed hard to the back of his teeth, his stomach roils. "What, am I not s'posed to be nice to her?" he snaps. "She's like one of those dogs—the small ones—who get their heads stuck in the tissue box. Need I remind you all my experiences have been with women who are *nothing* like Sophie Davis?"

For an endless minute, all of them are quiet. Liam knows better than to know it's over. He'd never make it that easy for any of them. Masochistically, he wants the same from them. There's been a distance that's been growing between the lot of them lately. The occasional consequence of growing pains within adult friendships between men who've known each other forever. This feels more even. They'd all been here, at one point or another in time.

Eventually, it's Noah who dares to counter: "What if that's the point, Liam?"

What if? echoes through his mind. Bouncing off the walls of his head like the rubber ball Sophie had bought 'their' puppy. Liam doesn't find those two words playful at all. They're chilling. Painful, sometimes. They invite opening boxes he's long since shut and stowed in the back of his closet. Never to be looked at, and still carried to every new place he ever lives. *What if* invites summoning ghosts from loves long lost; some who'd deserted him, some banished, and some who held on so tightly they broke him.

There had been Sadie, who'd been underneath the bleachers, laughing raucously and doing things that could've gotten her suspended. The first girl he'd ever thought himself in love with. She'd been free, too. She looked like what he'd imagined freedom must. With her wild hair and wilder joy. Too wild, joyful, and free to commit to a life in this small town. Liam, unfortunately, was this small town. So there that had ended.

Then there had been Georgia. Ethan called her an overcorrection. Liam had called her the love of his life for two years. His vicious, ambitious career woman. She'd gone from a debate star in high school to a shark in the courtroom in record time. He had learned a lot from her. Like discipline and drive. Pride and the power of putting money where your mouth is. Then she'd taught him loving someone wasn't the same as understanding them. It definitely wasn't the same thing as respecting them.

Lessons he'd taken into his relationship with Dina when he'd met her in a bar. She was always having the most fun in every room. Between Sadie's untethered selfishness and Georgia's belittling ambition, Dina had felt like a happy middle. It had only been after months of his life wasted, and her leaving him a brief but crushing email telling him he was too boring for her, that Noah had told him he wasn't Goldilocks and he couldn't just pick a middle-ground girl who was *just right*.

When he thinks about it now, it doesn't sting as much. That surprises him. Though, not as much as it surprises him to puzzle out that Sophie had pieces of what attracted him to every single one of them —and then some.

Sophie's laughter was infectious, more genuine and freely given than anyone else's. She wasn't one to keep joy to herself. Yet Liam's found himself no less thirsty for it. Sophie's driven and passionate, but never selfish. She adapts to life's challenges with a grace that Liam himself struggles to match. She accommodates. She cares, so deeply. Liam almost can't fathom how she holds all that care in such a little body. She says so many words, and her actions are still remarkably bold. Like the swift kick she'd land on his shin if she heard him call her body little. Like the way she'd dug her fingers into him when she'd pulled him into a hug last night.

She doesn't think he's boring. She asks him questions like the answers matter.

What if that's the point?

SOPHIE

Her stomach churns painfully until there's bile burning the back of her throat. It sits there, acidic. Blistering. Sour proof of her heart getting away from her again.

He'd called her a little dog with her head stuck in a tissue box. Pegged her as being nothing more than another damsel in distress. *Pathetic,* in so many words. It was one thing to feel it. It's a wholly surreal experience, Sophie discovers, to witness it being proclaimed to a handful of men who do not know you. By a man she'd thought had begun to. He hadn't helped her because he cared. He'd done it because he felt *sorry* for her. Because she was too soft for all of it.

What's worst of all is that she can't help but prove him right now. Sobbing on her bedroom floor, and there's nothing cinematic or pretty about it. Snot is sticky on her swollen lips, her cheeks feel raw with a blush that needles at her skin. The only mercy—and it's so small, she can't bear to be grateful for it at all—was that he hadn't seen her. He hadn't seen her listening. And she hadn't caught him speaking *after* she'd done what she'd shown up to do: Ask him to be her date to an event that was happening because of his faith in her.

She can't believe she'd begun to fall for him. She can't believe she's gone and done this to herself again. She'd romanticized his attitude. His sharp tongue and abrasive nature, she'd just reduced them to extraneous details—and *why?* All because she'd wanted to believe the best in him? Maybe it's her attachment to the idea of a *good man.* Or to what she's wanted this town to be to her. No matter which way she turns it, all she can think is he has a point. She *feels* pathetic. Something the other women he's dated never were. Just like he'd said to his buddies.

Just thinking about it, Sophie tries to laugh. It comes out in a wail instead.

———

Now and again, life affords people choices. Or subjects them to a fatal crossroads from which there's no turning back. It doesn't have to be that dramatic, of course. It can just feel that way. Either way, sometimes a girl's got to put on the dress and show up where she's promised to.

When the choice is between her heartache and something bigger, Sophie doesn't think it's a choice at all. Hearts heal. Deceptively fragile, and still so durable. There's poetry in stitches she's always been able to appreciate. Maybe it makes her more a fool than she feels like, contorting to zip up her own dress—but she's a durable fool.

She'll be in a dress that matches her convertible: a precious, lovely powder blue. There's no pinafore. But the tulle concoction is a flouncy dream with full, puffy sleeves that cinch at her wrists. It's demure in a way that its deep, plunging neckline and corset-style bodice contradict wickedly. She's swept her hair back with a black headband she's fashioned out of silk ribbon. It matches the dainty Mary Jane heels that encase her feet, already swathed in knee socks the sultry slit in the dress' side unveils.

Sophie holds fast to these details. Tries to take pleasure in them, like she can wipe from her mind the reason she'd been so excited to wear this dress. To pretend it had been for the theme after all, and not the person who'd been in-sync, deciding the theme with her.

It's impossible when Liam's the one who's brought her vision to life. He'd matched every dollar she'd put into setting it up, and had helped her fast-track vendors—and that had been *before* he'd corralled his friends to set it all up. How was she supposed to hate him? Whatever his intentions were, he'd helped. He'd helped her like her win was his win.

Need I remind you all my experiences have been with women who are nothing *like Sophie Davis?* Liam's voice echoes in her head, unbidden.

With her knuckles pressing to her sternum, she forces herself out of the car. She thinks, *His loss,* then tries her best to believe it.

A handful of people other than herself isn't the welcome distraction Sophie geared herself up to dive headfirst into. Even those four other people don't look thrilled to be there. In fact, she catches one glance at her furtively. She's almost certain they'll be gone within the next ten minutes, too.

Her bodice begins to feel suffocatingly tight, just standing here. Liam had kicked up such a fuss over her—on top of Colton vouching for her with *the mayor*—and now she wasn't just a joke and a failure. She was also the worst friend. An undependable one. No matter how deeply she kneads her knuckles into her tight chest, the pressure won't let up.

She can't bear to meet anyone's eyes.

But then, "Hey, Soph," sounds by the shell of her ear. Sophie hates that she knows that it's Liam the moment the sweet spice of cinnamon and spearmint envelopes her. One hug and deep inhale and her body memorized his smell. It isn't acceptable, that she doesn't jump or flinch; instead, despite his cruel words, the tension in her shoulders melts away.

She doesn't say anything when she turns. She doesn't have it in her to say anything. She doesn't trust her voice to stay steady. It already takes all her will to school her features into a neutral expression. She oscillates between daring her face and pleading with it to not give away the way her heart lurches at the sight of him. Liam Brooks on any ordinary day is a handsome devil. In a top-hat and deep purple waistcoat, he's just unfair.

And then, he has the audacity to ask her, "Will you dance with me?"

Behind him, a crowd floods the marquee. They wind their costumed bodies around trees bedecked in tinsel and tea cup ornaments. There are lawn gnomes reminiscent of Absolem—maybe even too many of them. Fairy lights swoop everywhere in sight, blinking merrily. Snow's begun to dust the ground outside like powdered sugar. She doesn't have to question it. These people didn't come for her. He's who they know, and he's who they did it for. It shouldn't matter to her, Sophie knows, so long as they contribute. Her plans would come to fruition, local businesses would thrive despite the economy; what does it matter, who gets the credit?

"How can I say no?" Sophie says—and she almost hopes he'll give her the answer.

Chapter Six

LIAM

She's always pretty, but tonight Sophie is stunning. Her blue dress highlights the pink in her cheeks and the warmth in her eyes.

He doesn't get to marvel for long.

As soon as she's in his arms, her face is tucked into his chest. Her forehead rests against the pale gold silk of his tie. He'd thought of her golden hair when he'd donned it, but he sees now that it is darker than her shade of blonde. "If I compliment this outfit, are you going to threaten to kick me again?" he teases, tugging her back to the very beginning. His head knows, technically, it's only been a matter of weeks. But his bones feel like they've known Sophie forever. Just being close to her is enough to flood them with warmth.

"No," she says quietly, not rearing back to look at him.

He hopes she's smiling, but her face gives nothing away. Unsure, Liam tries again with a light tease, "Okay, here goes: You look phenomenal, Sophie. More Cinderella than Tinkerbell. You can do it all."

She sounds so strained, and about as warm as the climate outside of the marquee, when she says, "Thank you." The sound is muffled by the fabric.

Of all the moves Liam would have expected himself to make,

wrapped so close to Sophie tonight, wrenching her body away from his wouldn't have even made it on the list. For most of the day, he's only thought about doing the very opposite. And still, here he is: his hands curling around her biceps to tear her away and hold her in place to look at. Like if he looks hard enough, he can see into her mind. The blank look on her face isn't Sophie Davis.

"Sophie, are you okay?" he tries again.

Sophie's expression remains unreadable, her voice flat. "Yes, thank you." She glances at his hands still holding her arms. "Are you done?" The sudden coldness in her tone stuns Liam, leaving him unsure of what caused the shift.

Liam blinks at her, slowly. His lips purse. "No. I'm not, actually. Though you clearly have something better to do," he jeers, taking his hands off of her. He holds them up against her, like he's holding her off. His countenance contorts to an ugly mockery of deference. "Go for it, Tinkerbell. Whatever your better offer is."

He swears he sees something actually flash in the depths of those eyes. She snaps, "*Don't* call me that!" If that doesn't remind him of when they'd first met, what could? "Oh, don't you dare– Don't you *dare* smile at me. Why do you like this? Why do you enjoy making me make a fool out of myself?"

Liam scoffs at the accusation. "You're never a fool. What on earth are you on about?"

"What—" Sophie cuts herself off, and he watches her, enraptured, try to hold herself back. He doesn't even know why she's trying to. He repeats his question, the syllables sharpened on the whetstone of his greed for the passionate, unfettered girl he's fallen for. She breaks like a dam: "I *like* you. I don't even know why, because you're insufferable. No one needs to be so moody and broody all the darn time. But hey, you're beautiful so it works, right? Maybe being mysterious is overrated, Liam. Have you ever thought about that? Maybe I *am* a puppy with my head in a tissue box – if the tissue box is some Schrödinger-adjacent metaphor for the *box* being *wanting to know how to make you laugh*. If it's thinking about your stupid *hands,* and your stupid hair, and your unfortunately memorable eyes, and—"

He doesn't find out what else had been on the list, because it's the moment Liam's mouth covers her. His palms cradle her soft, round jaw and he kisses her and kisses her and kisses her until he has to pull away for breath. Even then, panting, he has to tell her, "I like you, too. But I do know why. Because my dad told me once that sunflowers grow towards the sun. And when I think about that now, I think about you. Choosing the bright side like it's in your dominion. You're strong in ways I might never be. You're wonderful, Sophie. I just don't know why you're acting so weird tonight, like–"

"I'm *nothing* like the girls you've dated. You said– I heard you, before. I was coming to..." She swallows hard, and it ruthlessly yanks at his heartstrings to see her mouth, swollen from his kiss, downturned at the corners like this. "I heard you."

"You're not my type, Sophie," Liam tells her artlessly. It's the truth. Fortunately, he tells it to her with his hands still holding her close— because she immediately tries to make a run for it. Despite himself, Liam barks a laugh.

What if that's the point?

"*Sophie*. Soph– That's a good thing," he promises, his mouth brushing hers faintly. His eyes never leave hers. "You're not an archetype, Sophie Davis. You're an awakening." She's said enough, he thinks.

When she opens her mouth, inevitably to argue, he kisses her all over again.

Chapter Seven

"I NEVER TOOK you for a casual waver," Sophie muses, swinging their tangled hands between them. She's mostly leading. Despite her shorter legs, she's got the quicker stride. And maybe Liam just likes the view from a step behind her.

He smiles to himself, confirming, "I'm not." His wave to Tyler Reed in passing, while he'd chuckled away on the phone looking besotted, wasn't camaraderie at its finest. Being happy just makes him obnoxious, Liam's found.

"But you just—" Sophie begins to argue, and Liam drags her into his side, squeezing her there. He explains, "Sometimes I do it to catch people off-guard. I don't go around smiling at everyone either. But when you're already making me smile, and people are in my path, there's nothing I can do about that, is there? It's become fun."

Sophie has to reach up on tip-toe to press her icy lips to Liam's cold cheek, but his hold keeps her steady when she attempts it while walking. "Did I tell you the mayor's office finished counting the donations from the drive?"

He nuzzles the tip of his nose against her feathering hairline. "You know you didn't, sweetheart. How'd we do? Can you afford me yet?"

She laughs her bright, raucous laugh, pinching his side. "We went over the forecasted number, actually," she tells him proudly. It's a pride the brilliant curve of his mouth effuses, too. "Though, I guess we're just cycling it. What're you going to spend all that money on besides taking me on dates?"

"How about the dog you conned me into getting?" Liam provokes.

Sophie sticks her tongue out at him. "He conned you himself. I just opened the door, remember? But whatever– I can live with that. Especially because I can't wait to get more. The shelter always needs more help, and I know you didn't believe it then, but I hope you do now, baby. You would be so good there."

Liam can't even pretend to be peeved. His girlfriend and her heart— the one she's let him have and hold and care for. He shoves open the door to the diner, where his friends sit in a group he doesn't join as the fifth wheel this time. He has Sophie, and he'll be keeping her forever.

He tells her, "We'll see." But there isn't a person here who doesn't know he'll never deny her anything. He could never, ever want to.

The End.

Sweet Deal

Chapter One

TYLER

Tyler Reed hears too often, *"You should get out more."* Solicitous inflections of, *"You're too much of a homebody."* And other variations of the sort. Some days it's more hassle than it's worth to explain that he's seldom got more of a reason to go out than stay in, given his job. It would be hard to run an IT company without IT, wouldn't it?

He can't run it so successfully without Noah Harrison's UX consultancy, either.

Consequently, that evening, when Noah invites him to hang out at the Sip 'n Saw bar in the middle of town, Tyler agrees gamely. In hindsight, maybe he should've asked some questions before hanging up the phone.

It might have prepared him for the group the bar's door opens to. Maplewood Grove is too small a town for him not to know each of them. Knowing Ethan Parker (reticent town mechanic), Alex Carter (Ethan's cousin – maternal, teacher), and Liam Brooks (Ethan *and* Noah's best friend, renowned contractor) doesn't quell Tyler's unease. Not that it keeps him from venturing forward, regardless.

Noah's dark blond head snaps to attention, not unlike an excitable golden retriever. "Tyler!" he exclaims. His enthusiasm would be better suited to a long-lost brother; Noah had come over to his place only yesterday. Tyler's had months of working together to acclimate to Noah's easy warmth, though. Its familiarity sets him at ease.

He grins back, meaning it. "Evening, gents." He flashes a peace sign. It feels ridiculous, but it isn't like he can think of a cooler greeting. Noah's quick to hug him, clapping a hand to his back—before ruffling his curls with the same hand. "Ty, these are the boys. Ethan—don't take it personally, he doesn't get chatty with everyone and he doesn't mean to look like someone took a piss in his Cheerios; that's just his face. Liam- Man, I'm already sorry for him. Don't take anything he says to heart. He's all bark, I promise. And Alex... is... the best."

The tawny-haired teacher (*Science?* Tyler tries to place) nods with a bright smile. "It's true. I totally am. And it's not just the English teacher stereotype." (*Whoops, close enough.*)

"Hey, dude," Liam says. "Noah raves about your big brain all the time. If you wanna help me hack into Harrison's bank account or something, it'd score you a bunch of points with me." The black-haired contractor flicks the back of Noah's head, but he offers Tyler his fist to bump all the same.

An invitation Tyler accepts, though he guffaws, countering, "What about me says I'd do well in jail?" He gestures to himself, knowing not much more needs to be said about his lanky body. He is taller than everyone at the table—despite being younger than all of them, too—but there isn't much muscle definition going on here. Nothing like Ethan's bulging biceps or Noah's sculpted physique.

Alex's grin loosens further. "I like him," he decrees like that's all it takes. *Who knows? Maybe it does,* Tyler reasons. "We can keep 'im."

A beer plants itself in front of Tyler. He hadn't ordered one yet—and, to his surprise, it was Ethan who'd placed it there. He isn't done gaping when the mechanic shoots him a crooked smile and raises his own pint in a toast Tyler didn't earn. *Maybe this won't be too bad.*

"What were we talking about?" Liam interjects.

Noah summarizes, "You were whining about Sophie bringing home another stray and kicking Alex under the table for justifiably mocking you. I'd finished telling Ethan that Hannah's called dibs on pies for Thanksgiving, so tell Liv not to bother. Oh, and my baby sister's finally coming home from her post-graduation trip to Europe." Tyler deduces the rundown is for his benefit, and appreciates it.

Liam snickers, teasing, "In case you forgot, Noah's parents are loaded."

Alex elbows him noticeably. "That's gauche, dude."

Tyler laughs into his beer, absorbing the wordless kinship between the men—deceptively light, yet undeniably enduring.

"*Ho*-kay, English major," Liam hoots.

Somehow, all the chatter comes to an abrupt halt the moment Ethan clears his throat. It isn't a loud, condemning sound by any means. In fact, Tyler would call it gentle. Coaxing. Even nervous. Ethan speaks like he's ripping off a Band-Aid when he states, "I'm asking Olivia to marry me." Liam's subsequent choking on a sip of his drink punctuates the moment. Alex's eyes go wide as saucers.

Tyler looks at Noah and finds his head tilted. His ear almost brushes his shoulder. Tyler's never seen Noah sound so serious as when he asks: "Are you sure?"

All it takes is a solid, unhesitating nod from Ethan and Noah grins. "Congratulations, then. You're a lucky man."

"You're a lucky— *Congratulations?!*" Liam splutters, swatting at Alex's arm attached to the hand that pats frantically at his back. Tyler can't blame Alex for finding the look of unadulterated alarm funny. He watches him stumble over a laugh and then watches it earn Alex a withering scowl from Liam's icy blue eyes.

Yikes, Tyler flinches. Noah's quick to sling an arm around his shoulders, patting his arm.

"Don't," Noah says to Liam.

Liam is undeterred. "That's nuts, Ethan!" he argues, palm slapping the table. "You've barely been dating her for a year. She's great, sure! But why the rush?"

To Ethan's credit, he doesn't look fazed. He takes a swig of his beer, cool as a cucumber. "When you know, you know." He shrugs. Noah hadn't exaggerated. He's a man of few words. The look of disbelief on Liam's face elicits more, though. "Life's too short, man. She moved here when her grams died. My old man, healthy as a darn horse, who hadn't smoked a cigarette in his life, got lung cancer and died before he hit sixty. I love her. I want to make her my wife *yesterday*."

Tyler doesn't care if it earns him a glare of his own. Ethan's speech deserves a slow clap, he thinks; why wouldn't he give it one? He does. Noah and Alex are quick to join in. Liam snorts at them, and some friction dissipates.

It bolsters Tyler, that he makes a corner of Liam's mouth twitch upwards before he huffs, "My girlfriend would like you."

Tyler quips, "Good taste."

He can feel eyes on the side of his head. He doesn't expect Ethan's dark gaze to be the subject. It is, though. Tyler's head can't help but turn. Fortunately, he isn't in the middle of a sip when Ethan asks, "Have you ever been in love, Tyler?" He could've choked on his beer, too. As it is, he does choke on air.

"Uh, yeah—once?" Tyler scrambles. The spotlight isn't where he thrives in the first place. Beneath Ethan's gaze, the focus is piercing; it doesn't leave a choice for much else besides the truth. So, he admits, "But it was enough for me to respect what it can do."

GRACE

Everything about the woman in the mirror is purposefully soft. From the glowy, minimalist makeup in a muted mauve spectrum to the dark curls left loose to frame her features. The subdued lavender of the cardigan donned over the cream silk blouse tucked into her flowy tan skirt. Her jewelry is simple, traditional—small baubles of gold, never crossing the line from sophisticated to flashy.

She planned every bit of it out. Half of the items don't even belong to her, but she happens to have the best friend on the planet. "*You've got this,*" Grace Thompson insists to her reflection.

Unfortunately, nothing can be done about the sharp, shrewd obsidian of her eyes. There's no replacement. No amount of pastel eyeshadow softens it. She can only hope her presentation is too riveting for Margaret Harper, CEO of Harper & Co., to notice. *Maggie,* she reminds herself. It doesn't matter that it feels unprofessional and way too casual to her ear. What the powerhouse prefers, the powerhouse gets. One has to earn the right to make their own rules. She isn't there yet. She's paying her dues. Hence the manufactured details that are all part of her pitch.

These semantics shouldn't matter, Grace thinks—but she knows they do. She can't change the way the world works, not if she wants to be successful in it. This want is unconditional. Today, it brings Grace to the five-minute mini-meltdown in the bathroom of Harper Co.'s building she's scheduled in.

A stopwatch runs on her phone, balanced on the sink's ceramic lip. She demands her breaths to even out. She's practiced this. She knows everything there is to know about this company.

Harper & Co.: a family-owned business that specializes in organic and sustainable products. Spearheaded by Chief Executive Officer, the forty-three-year-old maven, Maggie Harper. Maplewood Grove native, who still ran her operations out of the small town. Her company is operational all over the country. She values the planet, and community, and consistently puts her money where her mouth is. Only one of many examples is her continued support of the Maplewood Grove Thanksgiving Parade. This year, she's a major sponsor. She's notoriously exacting. Incredibly picky about who she allows into the company she runs like her family. Her company's growth has plateaued for this very reason, and no one around her has the guts to say so.

Grace does. Not only does she possess fortitude in spades, she also has a strategy to start turning things around before the last quarter is over. She's good at what she does. She respects Maggie's mission and wants to help it be even more successful. She has a well-devised strategy, backed by endless research. Statistics and figures. Pretty pie charts, too. There's no way Maggie won't see it. *Right?* The woman in the reflection nods gamely back at her.

Grace shuns the anxiety puckering her mouth.

"—So, to reiterate," she concludes, clearing her throat, "you're leaving money on the table. This could be a huge opportunity for you. Marketing doesn't have to be sleazy and disingenuous to be effective. If you allow me the opportunity, I'd love to be the one to spearhead the growth strategy for your awesome business, Maggie." *There,* Grace exhales. *For better or for worse, done.*

With a final press on her presentation clicker, Grace braves a look at the woman in charge. She hates to feed into a sexist stereotype, but Maggie doesn't look it. Dressed in a sweater set in deep burgundy, and shoes that Grace thinks deserve to be called *clogs.* Her dark skin glows, and she wears her hair in long braids down her back. She looks like she's about to bake cookies, not issue a mandate for her million-dollar company. How many other titans and moguls has she met who radiate such warmth?

It kills Grace, how badly she wants this woman to like her.

"Honey," Maggie's voice is scratchy in the most comforting way. "Why don't you sit down?" Unfortunately, the look on her face is not.

To Grace, it looks almost pitying. Her stomach roils in distress. She doesn't want to *sit down.* She wants to run away. She wants control—over time, so she can go back to fifteen minutes ago and give a different speech, and over her body, so she can extinguish the mortified heat that floods her face. Of course, she sits down anyway.

Maggie says, "You've got wonderful ideas here, Grace. I believe I can speak for all of us—" she gestures broadly at the other Harpers around the conference table, "—when I say the depth of your research is impressive. Maybe a little scary, but..." Even Grace can't help but titter at that. It sounds pathetic to her ear. Nothing that comes after '*but...*' is ever pleasant. No matter how kind Maggie's smile, that's still true. She tries not to hold her breath too noticeably, watching the other shoe drop in slow motion. "You talk a lot about profits, and that's great. I'm not naive; I know it's crucial for the business. But here in Maplewood Grove, these holidays—like Thanksgiving—mean something more. They're about bringing the community together, celebrating the ties that bind us. The parade isn't just an event; it's a tradition that keeps this town's spirit alive. It's a time when everyone, from the youngest kids to the oldest residents, comes together. Profits are important, but they should come as a result of that spirit, not at its expense."

"I *know*," Grace blurts. Her own eyes widen at her interruption. Never, not once in her life, has she been so rude as to interrupt anyone, let *alone* a prospective client who was older than her, who'd done more than paying her dues, and was someone she personally admired. She doesn't know what to do. Maggie doesn't even look affronted; she looks *curious*. Grace has to keep going. Keep going with *what?!* Her mouth decides for itself: "I understand. But there should be no reason two things can't coexist. Despite the messy history this holiday has, I do appreciate what it's come to stand for. Gratitude and community and— and *pie*. My boyfriend makes a killer pie. I look forward to it all year!" It's a good thing this woman doesn't know Grace beyond her credentials. Or else she'd know just how uncharacteristic it is, the way she claps her hands together in sponged excitement.

Maggie Harper has moved on to looking amused. Her warm, chocolate eyes seem to shine with humor. Like she knows Grace is lying, but still really wants her to pull this off. "Is that right?" she asks, grin almost playful.

"I can bring him. I, um— How about we table this discussion for now, and you just get to know me?" Grace insists, on a roll now; full steam ahead! "I can help you build your float for the Thanksgiving Parade this year. My boyfriend will make his special pie. And we'll... see?"

For a long, torturous moment, no one says anything at all. Grace has never been a fan of hyperbole or unnecessarily poetic metaphors—but she understands, now, how silence can be *deafening*.

"Okay," Maggie agrees. She says it so quickly, Grace isn't sure she hasn't imagined it. Fortunately, she has some mercy and continues, "I'm not promising anything, to be clear. But we can see."

Grace can only count it as a victory that she doesn't fall out of her chair. "*Awesome!*" she exclaims. The sound is like a cheerleader's fist pumping in the air. "I get it. Totally. I— Really, thanks, Maggie!" The irony isn't lost on her, given her name, how gracelessly she grapples.

Meanwhile, a single question blinds her like a neon sign: *Where on EARTH do I find a serious, pie-making boyfriend in three days?*

Chapter Two

GRACE

There is a bottle of red wine propped atop her midsection. She's still in her cream blouse. It's fine. Apparently, Grace's mouth has decided she's a daredevil. The first twenty-six years of her life notwithstanding, obviously.

"*Why*," she bemoans to the ceiling. The ceiling, because she can't bear to lift her head and whine to the redhead fiddling around in their kitchen. If Grace thought her name felt painfully ironic that day, then at least Hannah Baker—her best friend, yes, but also a *baker*—made her feel better. Just being in Hannah's ambit achieves that, though. It isn't her fault that Grace has dug herself into a hole too deep to leap out from.

Still, she makes a valiant effort to throw Grace some rope. If rope were made of apple crumble and vanilla ice cream. Both made from scratch. Not to mention free as Hannah's belly-laugh, soothing. "Your instincts helped you out. This isn't a *bad* thing. It may not be the most convenient, but it isn't over till it's over, Grace! Have a little faith."

"Running low," Grace grumbles despondently. "I'm having wine instead."

"Then soak it up with some of this," Hannah cajoles, her voice closer now. Grace lifts her heavy head from the ground to see the red-haired angel place a cork trivet atop the cheap ramshackle coffee table they'd put together their first night living together – eons ago, now. She places a dish on top of it. The warm, sweet, cinnamon-laced smell of the dessert almost makes Grace's eyes water.

Too solemnly, she declares, "I love you. *You* should be my boyfriend."

Hannah takes it as a sign to pluck the bottle from her body. *Probably wise,* Grace thinks. "I could try, but I don't think Mrs. Harper would be convinced," Hannah reasons, too reasonably. "Besides, Noah's too well-known. It's Maplewood Grove. You can't live here for an extended period of time and not know who's an item."

Grace looks to her best friend with as much distaste as she can muster with a watering mouth. "I can't believe you just unironically referred to yourself and your boyfriend as an *'item.'* Friendship over, I think." There's no heat to the words. In fact, Grace suspects her point is lost when her head thumps back on the rug.

She can still hear the sunny grin in Hannah's voice, bathing syllables in warmth. "Then who will give you a fantastic idea that'll save face in front of this lady you've been hero-worshiping?" she baits.

It's a cheap shot. Grace counters, "Let me guess! You're gonna let me borrow Prince Charming for a week?"

She's known Hannah for years. They may not have found each other in the most conventional way possible; Grace's initial roommate had skipped town to move with her boyfriend to San Francisco, and she'd run into a merry, magnetic redhead who made it all feel fated. Technically, Hannah is older. She feels younger than Grace has ever felt. It's why it startles her when Hannah argues, with a rare edge to her words, "Absolutely *not.*" Somehow, it's still *so Hannah* that she apologizes a second after. "Oops. Green eyed monster, sorry!"

Grace snorts, holding up a thumbs up like a white flag. "Still love you."

"*Good,*" Hannah stresses. "Remember that in a second, 'kay? Because my fantastic idea *is...* Tyler. You're— Hold on!" Emphatically, she claps her hands together. Grace realizes in retrospect who she'd borrowed her movements from during her meeting with Maggie. She can't interrupt Hannah after that; her mouth closes as quickly as it had opened. "You're friends. You're always telling me you're still friends. You said it wasn't weird that he works with Noah because you are. Amiable split and all? I know we're friends and I'd do it for you. Shouldn't the same hold true for him?"

She stares at the ceiling harder. "No."

"Why not?"

Grace huffs, forcing her body into a semi-vertical position. Her palm slaps down on the table for support, keeping her steady while she blinks at Hannah. "It's *weird,*" she says, like it's obvious. It is. Isn't it?

"So is lying to a prospective client about a pie-baking boyfriend so she'll hire you." Hannah beams angelically.

Grace holds out her hand, demandingly. "Give me back the wine and no one gets hurt."

"Call Tyler and I will." Sweet but firm. She won't budge.

Not that Grace is under any illusions she's going to win this. What is there to win? Feeling not unlike a petulant toddler, she harrumphs. Even with the peripheral edges of her perception softened, she knows she doesn't have another choice.

The only other option would be to admit to Maggie Harper that she's a liar and a sore loser... Get potentially blackballed in the industry she's dedicated herself to... Be a joke. So, there's really only one option, isn't there?

Better than no options, Grace weakly yields. "Dial. Please."

Hannah doesn't say a single word. She's a better person than Grace is, she thinks. Some of Grace's favorite words have always been *I told you so.* Hannah, on the other hand, thumbs her way through Grace's phone, and hands over a ringing line. **TYLER REED** emblazoned on the screen. There's no contact picture anymore. His face had once had Grace's lips attached to it.

She doesn't expect it to ring for long. It doesn't. Four rings, and his voice pours down the line. Gruff-sounding, as if from disuse. "Grace? Everything good?"

She takes it off speaker, though she doesn't protest when Hannah squeezes in closer, pressing her ear to the other side of the phone. Warm vanilla envelopes her with the baker's closeness. Grace breathes easier—

easy enough to quip, "Does something have to be wrong for me to call? You're my friend."

Tyler's laughter sounds nervous. She's probably projecting. "I am, yeah," he says agreeably, confirming her theory. "Let me try this another way: What's up, pal?"

"*Pal?*" she giggles. *Too much wine,* she thinks.

"Friends say 'pal.' I've heard." When you've known someone as long as she's known him, you don't have to see them to know the look on their face. Sometimes, you can hear it. Grace can, just then. She can hear Tyler's dopey, crooked grin. His mop of curls falling in his eyes. His body half-slouched.

She flinches as Hannah's elbow digs into her side, her eyes locking onto Hannah's with a mix of annoyance and amusement. Despite herself, she rolls her eyes, a smile breaking through her irritation. Defiantly, she suggests, "Fine, *pal.* Want to grab lunch tomorrow?" Her hand blocks Hannah's from grabbing the phone. She doesn't doubt her ability to hijack the situation—like Grace needs this situation to get any more mortifying than it already is.

Tyler's quiet for only a beat. Grace thinks she can hear him typing in the background. Unlike she once had, she doesn't take offense to it now. It isn't her business. She's just glad he answered the phone. Not every ex-boyfriend would have... not that Grace has very many—or, uh, *any*— to compare him to. She doesn't need to in order to understand Tyler's affable friendship is a rare gift. "Why don't you come over for dinner?" He puts down a counteroffer, then sweetens the deal, knowing her too: "I'll cook for you. Lasagna good?"

It's her favorite. He knows this. He knows she knows that he knows this.

Her grin feels dopey, too. "I'll see you at seven-thirty, pal."

TYLER

He isn't the kind of man with an inflated sense of self-importance. If he were, Tyler may have concluded that he'd tempted the universe. Instead, he is a man of numbers and odds. Probability. Coincidence, chance, circumstance.

There wasn't a conclusion, but a question: What were the *odds* of Grace Thompson, once upon a time love of his life... turned friend, calling him the very day he'd mentioned her in passing? Not zero. Never zero.

Tyler won't think about it any deeper than that. There's nothing to be gained from it. He's never needed to learn a lesson twice. There's proof in how he remembers to keep his phone in hand and follow the recipe closely. He gets more credit for the cooking than deserved, he thinks. All he does is follow instructions. He's not too rigid to not taste-test and make adjustments where his palette insists. For a brain like his, so often functioning in binary, he guesses that's the most surprising part of it.

What isn't a surprise is that his buzzer buzzes at seven-thirty-five. He doesn't have to look at his watch to confirm this, although he does. These are what he calls *Graceisms*. She is always, always on her own kind of *on time*: it's annoying to be too on time and disrespectful to be later than ten minutes. She won't take the elevator, despite Tyler's apartment being on the sixth floor. She'll check her step count on the fancy, cali-brating watch wrapped around her dainty wrist. Like a little kid, she'll grin like she's won a potato sack relay.

With a last peek at the oven door, making sure none of the cheese has dripped from the dish to the bottom, lest it fill his entire apartment with the odor of burnt cheese, he goes to wait in the doorway, propping himself up against the jamb. Like clockwork, Grace jogs up the stairs. She takes the last few two at a time. Her grin is sheepish when she catches him watching. In moments like these, Tyler forgets this isn't their normal anymore. Fortunately (or not), it takes only a moment to remember—where he *reminds himself* to remember—that he can't take her in his arms and kiss her hello. She won't warn him not to smear her lipstick, before pressing a second, softer kiss to his cheek.

She just wraps an arm around his neck; a half-hearted impression of intimacy. Not committing with both of them. Neither does she protest both of his arms overlapping at her waistline. One forearm stacked on top of the other. In tall heels, with her considerable height, they are almost the same height. "Hi," he murmurs, his lips brushing lightly against her temple before he reluctantly lets her go.

"Hello there," she says.

Grace steps into his apartment like she's done countless times before. Not for a while now, but – she'd been a regular, once. She still isn't a stranger, at least. "Get you something to drink?" Tyler offers. Not even when they'd been seriously dating had she been the sort to casually dip into someone's refrigerator. He wouldn't have cared. There was rarely much besides takeout and various beverages anyway. It wasn't formality that kept her from it, he didn't think. It was just... Another *Graceism*.

"Water?" She says it like a question.

He moves to get it. "Sure!" She doesn't come with him, like he'd expected. She seems rooted to her spot between his foyer and living room. Grace is never exactly the picture of ease, by nature. But she isn't typically so... *rigid* in the spine, either. She usually stands tall, with her narrow shoulders squared. Tyler remembers, because he remembers how she used to criticize his wayward slouch. Like he remembers how she hadn't, since the one time he'd snapped at her, in the early days of their strange friendship, telling her she wasn't his girlfriend anymore and didn't get to pick at him anymore. He can't *un*-notice it now. So much between them is unsaid. But it hasn't felt like she's literally biting her tongue for a long, long time. "D'you want to sit?" he prompts, trying to keep the unease from coating his syllables. He's mostly successful.

She looks at him strangely. Tyler didn't think Grace had any looks left she could give him that he couldn't identify the underlying emotion of. She still doesn't move to take a seat—though, after a stilted moment, she rounds his kitchen island to idle behind him. Grace Thompson is many things, but he's never seen her antsy. Or *quiet*, for that matter. It's what keeps their friendship afloat, he knows: her never letting it slip and fall stagnant in a ditch.

"You're being weird," he erupts. It sounds like an accusation he hadn't meant.

Grace's laugh doesn't sound like Grace's laugh. There's an edge to it —and, just looking at her, he can tell she heard it too. As if to say, *See?* his brows flit up his forehead. "*Ineedyoutopretendtobemyboyfriend,*" she spits out in a flurry. *Actually* spits. Bits of wet land on Tyler's cheeks.

"Huh?"

"Oh, God– I'm sorry. I'm *sorry,*" she gasps. Then, like she's making up for her sluggish pace before, she moves swiftly. Ripping off a paper from the kitchen roll, she hands it to him, waving it with an almost comically desperate look on her face. "I need— I *know* I sound like a whackjob, but I need you to pretend to be my boyfriend. And bake a pie. For a client. Please."

Tyler had always thought it was an expression, when people said *jaw dropping* shock. Apparently not. His jaw does, in fact, drop. He feels like a cartoon, his features more animated than he knows what to do with. "Wh– *Huh?*" he repeats, and it comes out sounding strangled. Not that he can be blamed. Surely, he's not the unhinged one here.

"I'm sorry—"

Even now, his body rejects the look on her face. She may not be his significant other, but she can't not be significant to him. They may have lost the stamp of a relationship status. It may even be for the best. (The probability is never zero.) Still, his emotions react to every single one that flits across her face. "Grace, stop apologizing!" he half-shouts, as panicked as her. "I'm just— I don't understand." What a feeble under-statement. He isn't sure this isn't some fever dream. His brain can't let go of that single word: *Boyfriend.*

"I know. I know, Tyler, we're just..."

"Is this a *joke?*"

Her face answers that for her. She looks sheepish—and this, too, is a disconcerting look on her. "No," she chokes out. "My work hasn't been doing the best. This client– It's *Maggie Harper,* Tyler. Signing her on would be a real turning point in my career. Except she thinks I don't have a life! Or a soul!"

Distractedly, Tyler holds out a water bottle to her. "You have a soul," he argues.

"Just not a life." Grace's mouth presses into a flat line of displeasure. "I didn't mean it like that—" Tyler starts to say, only to be cut off by her head shaking. She twists off the cap of her bottle, yet doesn't drink from it.

"I don't have a life," she states, matter-of-fact. "But I do have a brain, and it's good at this. I'm *great* at my job. And I made a stupid, desperate choice to keep her interested, because she was going to write me off. I've worked too hard to be written off now. You have no reason to do this for me, I know. I *know that*. But please do it anyway. You know I wouldn't ask you if I had another choice."

"Grace." He doesn't know why he says her name. It's just all he can.

She doesn't play fair. She tacks on another, "Please?"

"It'll be weird," he tries. Even he can hear what a miserable last ditch effort it is. His brain corrects: *It'll be a strange new form of torture, you mean.*

Really, he should know better. Grace doesn't have an overinflated sense of self either. She is good at her job. As good at it as she'd been good at school. It wasn't because she was born an effortless genius, or with some natural aptitude that had pushed her into corporate the way Tyler's professional journey had gone. She was the hardest worker he knew, even now. She's also a straight-shooter. It shouldn't surprise him when she shoots at him: "It could be a good use of the elephant in every room we're in. Tyler, I—I know our relationship didn't work out. I know I hurt you. I know you took the higher road, still being my friend. But you *are*. You are my friend. You're"—*the love of my life*, his heart suggests—"one of the few people in my life I can really, truly count on. I need this. I need a win so, so badly."

He's never been able to say *no* to her. He couldn't when they were seventeen and she said they should keep dating, that they could do long-distance. That it didn't matter if he didn't want to go to college like she did. He couldn't when she asked him to visit campus, and didn't come home for months, choosing internships over holiday breaks. He couldn't when she told him she couldn't do this anymore, that she loved him but she couldn't keep feeling like a bad girlfriend. And he couldn't when he'd run into her at the grocery store, their hands touching over the last can of the same awful energy drink they were both hooked on—and she'd said she'd rather split it than take it all. When she'd wanted to be friends, and the persistent ache in his chest quieted at the sight of her tiny, hopeful smile.

How can he start saying it now?

Chapter Three

WHEN TYLER'S phone first starts ringing, he doesn't register it as his ringtone, even though he's had the same one since he got this phone. To his hazy, watery subconscious, it's just distorted noise. Sharp, puncturing noise that startles him to wakefulness quicker than he's ready to come to.

He's done it to himself. Both with his propensity for losing things between the couch cushions, hence needing the ringer on in the first place, and the lethargy. He wouldn't be exhausted if he'd just gone to bed. Slept on it. Instead of dwelling and spiraling in wayward circles that have led him nowhere but right where he'd started, only dizzier.

His phone starts ringing all over again.

Grace's name is on the screen—in white block lettering over a photograph of her. Her head is thrown back in laughter, looking carefree. It's a rare sight. Always was, but it feels especially so nowadays. He chooses to believe that's why he's kept the picture display for the last five years – not everything has to be sentimental schlock.

Her words crack like a whip: "Are you still *asleep?*" Gone is the sweet, pleading Grace who'd left his head full as a hot air balloon. This one doesn't pause for his answer. (Which is fine, because he doesn't have one she'll like.) "I'm downstairs. Eleven-thirty, remember? We have to be at Maggie's by noon?" She gets shriller by the syllable.

Tyler forlornly imagines coffee in an I.V. "I'm up. I'm getting ready. Give me"—he peels the phone away from his cheek, confirming the time to be *eleven-twenty-three,* actually—"twelve minutes. That's five plus the seven you just lied about."

"Sorry not sorry," she harrumphs, and then hangs up. Tyler snorts, his pale fists scrubbing over his grossly dry, crusty eyes.

It shouldn't feel as strange as it does, for a part of Grace's life to be totally unknown to him. Based on the standard of traditional status quo between exes, it remains on par for her to reinvent herself in whichever direction she'd like. (Maybe he needs to stop falling asleep to legal dramas, as his own move of *reinvention.*)

Tyler isn't so backward a man, he doesn't think. This shouldn't be a hit to his ego. Yet here he is: stung. There is a laundry list of new things in her life, and Tyler finds his typical nonchalance missing in action when confronted with it.

She has on a perfume he's never smelled – something sweeter, floral, with a note of vanilla he would've never attributed to Grace. She has a new car, having replaced the beat up old Toyota Camry he'd helped her get with a *Volvo.* Silver. All Tyler can stupidly think is: just like Edward Cullen.

His stomach is a pit of dread; bottomless.

It doesn't help that she says nothing about his having taken a full fifteen minutes in his search for a clean shirt. Whatever the brittle smile she courteously bestows on him before handing over coffee is the very opposite of a *Graceism.* Tyler doesn't like anything about it. He knows he's wearing it on his face, too, when she starts talking to him about the weather.

"—predicting a snowstorm soon," she's telling the windshield. "I hope the snow comes quick if it's going to." *The weather,* Tyler thinks, exasperated. She's talking to him about *the weather.* He doesn't even know what to say in return. Again, fortunately, she doesn't wait for him to answer. Unfortunately, she shatters the silence by outright asking: "Everything okay?"

"I didn't sleep well last night." Tyler doesn't elaborate why not. Honestly, he doesn't think he has to. He knows he's right when she says, sounding the most herself she's done since he'd slid onto immaculate leather: "Thank you." Her hand slips from the gear shift to cover his, squeezing - only once.

He doesn't mean to, but he stiffens. Grace's hand doesn't linger too long after that. His eyes drift to her profile in time to see her head shake. He can see her lips purse before she reminds him, "We won't be able to sell this if you keep reacting like that. Are you sure you can handle this?"

Tyler had almost forgotten the competitive edge Grace could unearth from the depths of him. He doesn't ordinarily consider himself a competitive person. Sometimes, that changes; when it does, it takes a sharp turn. He rebuts, "Wouldn't have agreed if I couldn't, Gracie."

It's her turn to stiffen now. Unmissable. A perverse satisfaction burns in his belly. He doesn't want to ponder it any deeper than that. When Grace eventually, quietly suggests, "Should we have some ground rules? Just so no one gets hurt?" Tyler can tell she means him. There's precedent for it, but that doesn't matter. He stops feeling awful about satisfaction over making her squirm, for once.

He shrugs. "Sounds smart."

Grace nods to herself—and she looks plagued enough for him to not take it personally when she begins to rattle off ground rules Tyler doesn't believe, not for a second, she hadn't been waiting to bring up. Now *this*, he can objectively appreciate, is a Graceism. "We'll have to kiss. Couples kiss. But let's keep it to a minimum... on the mouth, I mean. Handholding is fine. Good. Casual touches were always more our thing anyway." She says it all like she's giving a presentation. All that's missing is a blazer and PowerPoint slides.

Tyler's laugh is strangled, more like a wince. "I remember," he says, the words heavy with unspoken regret, each syllable scraping like thorns caught in his throat.

GRACE

Maybe it *is* a little too creepy to divulge out loud... but she'd looked Maggie's house up on Google Earth. She knows her fear of being late by driving up to and idling in front of the wrong house is preposterous. But she self-soothes with evidence and nothing less.

Besides, it isn't like Grace is unhinged enough to think it'd help to add that the enormous house with its vast wraparound porch and green, green garden weren't done justice in grainy satellite imagery. She won't admit that her entire apartment is probably the size of one bedroom in this place. Then again, she hadn't thought she was unhinged enough to lie about a boyfriend. Or to ask her ex to masquerade in a role he hadn't played in half a decade. Yet here they are.

"Woah," Tyler breathes beside her. *Accurate.*

"Concurred."

"Do we just—?" Grace is already ringing the bell. "Okay then."

She doesn't get to review the ground rules with him one more time. Maybe she doesn't need to. A breath before the front door swings open, Tyler's palm takes a perch at the small of her back. It isn't Maggie who opens the door. It's her husband—a stocky, olive-skinned man, David Harper. Grace doesn't want to admit she knows that. Strategically, she introduces herself first, "Hey! I'm Grace Thompson. Is Maggie—?" David smiles at her, a knowing twinkle in his eyes.

"Come right on in." He gestures expansively with a sweeping hand. "And you must be Grace's boyfriend. My wife tells me you're going to be making us a very famous pie today. But no one's mentioned your name."

Grace's giggle comes out disastrously high-pitched. "Tyler. Tyler Reed."

Next to her, Tyler nods solemnly as he says, "Licensed to... grill."

Grace doesn't know whether to facepalm herself, or him. Before she reaches a verdict, David's meaty palm is slapping Tyler's back and ushering them inside. He doesn't introduce himself. The man and his wife have been in Forbes magazine before. She wonders if she should keep playing dumb, or give up the ghost.

It's a thought that is quickly drowned out approximately seven steps into the house: the sound of laughter, chatter, and movement is cacophonous. She can't help but shoot Tyler a look of concern. She'd given him a rundown on Maggie and her husband, their son, Damien, who was in law school. She hadn't gone into any more depth in that. She hadn't thought she needed to. Her instincts, once again, failed her. Somehow, it's Tyler's thumb that edges slow, soothing circles between the knobs of her spine. She almost forgets she'd been about to comfort *him.*

But she doesn't get a chance to broach the topic. All it takes is stepping into the expansive living room at the heart of the home—all warm colors and gratuitous decoration—before Maggie appears from the side. "Grace!" she exclaims, like they're old friends.

Tyler bows his head to Maggie, and holds out his hand to shake. "I'm Tyler Reed, ma'am. Where do I make these pies? My girl says I've got to knock your socks off or it's the doghouse for me." This time, when Grace laughs, she means it. A good thing, too, because she can *feel* Maggie watching her in peripheral view.

"Pumpkin," Grace agrees.

Tyler teases, "Yeah, sweetheart?"

The banter feels so casual, so *normal,* Grace sinks into it. She'd almost forgotten Tyler could do this, when she gave him a chance to. Just... Even her out, like he was the antidote. Soothe her, without evidence. With a playful aplomb that doesn't at all resemble her own recipe of calm, cool confidence—usually, at least. It's a pleasant surprise to pivot and find Maggie beaming at her, pleased.

"Well, we keep our dogs indoors, so you're welcome to stay even if your pies aren't up to scratch," Maggie teases. "Why don't you go on in? David'll be your sous chef. I can't cook for the life of me, either. My husband has all the culinary skills in our relationship."

Grace feels a pang of surprise, her forehead scrunching in astonishment. She never expected to have anything in common with someone like Maggie. As Tyler gives her a reassuring squeeze and wanders off, Grace tries to quell her sheepishness. It's a reminder that appearances can be deceiving; she had always assumed that Maggie, with her sweatersets and warm demeanor, was as much a domestic goddess as she was a successful businesswoman.

It's hard not to be aware of her own wrongness. She feels – young. Younger than she looks, and maybe even younger than she is. Less Grace Thompson: Marketing Machine. More... Grace Thompson, first Thompson to go to college. Who'd grown up in a sullen, miserable house, who'd scratched and clawed her way past a fate of poverty and strife. She knows, from what she's pored over, that it isn't that far a departure from how Maggie herself had started out. It's the first time she's felt self-conscious of how little time she's spent out of the mess she'd been born right into, though. "We're not intruding, are we?" Grace asks, and it's the most honest she's been with this woman since they'd met. "I know I invited myself over, technically. But..."

"You were being assertive," Maggie says, matter-of-fact. Her face doesn't give anything away, leading Grace out the sliding glass door to the backyard where she can see all sorts of float-making paraphernalia strewn about.

"I was trying," Grace agrees, finding honesty easier without Maggie's eyes on her.

"I didn't mind it. But that isn't to say I don't enjoy, too, seeing you like this."

Confusion distorts Grace's controlled tenor. "Like what?"

For a brief instant, Maggie doesn't answer. Grace considers whether she didn't speak loudly enough, that maybe Maggie thought *she'd* ignored her. As if she could ever. And then, the older woman tells her, "Open. Shieldless."

If Grace were someone who attributed anything in life to fate, she might have said it's what reels her eyes to Tyler. From the backyard, there's a clear view into the kitchen. His mop of curls falls into his eyes, and he shakes his head to get them out. Like a puppy. But she's a woman who puts all her stock in the work she puts in. In effort and strategy and discipline.

Open, Maggie'd said. *Shieldless.*

Grace had been just that, once. It had made her heart ache too much —too distractingly. That is why this is pretend. Why it will stay that way, no matter how wholly some knot inside her unspools at the sight of his pleased grin, watching him making David laugh at something Grace knows, without hearing a word, is ridiculous.

But she isn't unhinged enough to say any of this out loud.

This once, her mouth complies.

Chapter Four

GRACE

Grace wakes up and her body aches from the hours she'd put into building the float late into the night. There's a satisfied smile on her lips, all the same. She's never minded putting work into a worthwhile cause. *No pain, no gain* may be a cliché—but it's one for a reason. She stretches her arms over her head like a cat, sauntering across her bedroom (all four steps it took) to the window. She throws open the curtains.

That's all it takes for her smile to evaporate. Her breath condenses against icy glass. Even blurred, she can see the entire parking lot blanketed in snow. Inches and inches worth of snow. Her mood sinks like a boulder to the bottom of a lake.

The forecast had betrayed her. She'd checked—double-, no, *triple-*checked. *Light, potential snowfall. An inch or two. The weather would hold out, no matter how gray the sky.* The weatherman had made many predictions. Even before Grace turns on the news, her knuckles blanching from her grip on the remote control, she knows this is catastrophic.

It's confirmed in minutes. All Grace hears is excerpts of words all synonymous with *bedlam* to her. "Impassable roads" and "difficult, if not impossible, for participants and spectators to reach the parade route" and "heavy snow threatens to collapse floats." There is a vein in her forehead that protrudes when she's anxious. Pulses, throbbing visibly. Her fingertips press down on it—almost punishing.

Hannah isn't home. Last night, Grace hadn't cared. She'd been walking on air, practically. Now, she needs her. She needs—

A fist pounds at the door. Maybe Grace *would* start putting stock in fate.

She trips over her socked feet, rushing to the door. Her eyes are still bleary from sleep. They widen at the sight of Tyler in her doorway. In a beanie with... what she's pretty sure is the Bat Signal on it. "Wh—" she doesn't get past that. Belatedly, it strikes her: Hannah has keys to *their* apartment. Why would she have knocked?

"I saw the snow. I knew you'd panic. So, hi." He actually waves at her.

Defensively, Grace questions, "Since when do you wake up earlier than I do?"

He isn't fazed. He walks right on in like it's his own place, pulling his silly hat off his wild hair only to muss it further. "I knew you'd panic," he repeats.

"I'm not panicking. I was listening to the weather channel. The snow has stopped. All the damage that was going to happen is done. Now, it's about what I can do to fix it—as quickly as possible."

"We," Tyler corrects gingerly.

"How?" Grace demands, not unkindly. Only taking the reins, like they're the last tether to her sanity. They may well be. They're enough to keep her upright when it's Tyler who has the game plan. She'd never thought plans were his thing.

At some point, Tyler pulls out a laptop from a backpack Grace hadn't noticed.

"I've set up a communication network," he says casually, as if it's the simplest thing in the world. Between flipping the omelet he's frying for her, Tyler keeps typing away with his non-dominant hand.

"It loops in us, the mayor, and the Harper & Co. team. So, you don't have to scramble trying to contact multiple people. We just send out one update, and it'll go out to everyone you want to keep informed and updated."

Grace blinks at him, astonished. Tyler shoots her a grin that's almost bashful. His head ducks. Somehow, he still sounds a little smug when he mocks, "What, is it that surprising that I'm good at something too?"

TYLER

He can't deny that it's gratifying to render Grace speechless.

For as long as he can remember, it's been him who's been awe- and, consequently, dumbstruck. The shoe's on the other foot now. Instead of a liability, he's an asset. Tyler catches Grace's approving smile, a gesture that makes him feel unexpectedly warm. Grace's playful nudge doesn't escape him, but he pretends not to notice, savoring the rare moment of unspoken camaraderie.

He hadn't rescued her, because Grace didn't need rescuing. That's not who she is; it's never been who Tyler's needed her to be. But... he helped. Incontestably. He's worked alongside her, helped rally people to agree to spend tomorrow morning shoveling snow. It's Thanksgiving, and the list of people to thank has been growing all day. If all goes as slated, the route should be clear by the time afternoon rolls around. With it, like no hitch ever occurred, the parade could go on.

It isn't any of that which has him grinning ear-to-ear. There are no Harpers watching—and Grace still sits with the entire length of her arm pressed to his. She doesn't have to raise her voice above its tender murmur when she admits, "This is nice." Not entirely sure something stupid won't come out of his mouth if he opens it right this second, Tyler simply pushes his shoulder against hers in response. It must be enough for her. Grace adds, "Do you remember when—when I was in second year, and you used to drive up to me? We made that ramen—"

"—using water from the kettle your roommate snuck into the dorm," Tyler finishes without hesitation. "Yeah. Of course I remember."

For some reason, that pinches an eleven between her elegant brows. Grace is the only person whose mind he's ever wanted to read. With most other people, it sounds like a way to hurt yourself. Maybe Grace is the only one he already knows is worth the pain. Hasn't the worst already happened? They've gone from adolescents to adults. So much time, gone.

"Does it make you mad at me, to think about that stuff?" she asks. Never, not in a million years, could he have predicted this was on her mind. Another *Graceism*: She keeps him on his toes. He doesn't bother to pretend he isn't taken aback.

Gently, he checks, "Because you broke up with me not long after, you mean?" Tyler feels her nod more than he sees it. It's probably a good thing he can't look at her right now, for both their sakes. "That would be like hating you for the very reason I fell in love with you, Grace. You always had such a good head on your shoulders. I was all over the place, but not you. You were—" He laughs, but he doesn't know why. Not really. There's nothing funny about it at all. "Don't get me wrong, it was painful. It hurt for a long time. But I also know you, and your good head and your good heart, and I know you wouldn't have made the choice if you didn't genuinely believe it was the best choice to make."

He can sense her tears without even turning to look, a knot tightening in his chest. Every fiber of him wants to reach out, to soothe, but something holds him back—a mix of fear and desire, swirling and colliding, leaving him paralyzed.

Without turning his head, he jostles her with another nudge. "Besides," he forces levity in, "this isn't so bad, is it?" He has to look when he can tell she's looking at him. She has those eyes: discerning, mythic.

Her smile tightens around his heart, a vise-like grip that he feels deep in his chest. The memory of her touch lingers, ghosting over his skin. How much longer can he pretend that the yearning that keeps him awake at night isn't real? Finally, she whispers, "No. It's not so bad."

Chapter Five

TYLER

Tyler is still half-dreaming of lemonade in July when he stirs.

Frazzled, dark strands tickle his nose till it's scrunching. Somewhere, in the recesses of his mind, it's still summer five years ago. He still has the girl, and she still loves him back. Her body, hot and bathed in gold beneath the irreverent sun, fits against his like a puzzle piece.

It isn't a dream. Just a memory. From so long ago, it may as well belong to someone else.

When he comes to and finds Grace in his arms, it strikes like lightning. He jolts—truly, physically *jolts* away in shock. Not because it feels wrong, but because it has to be. In the depths of her slumber, her fingers curl into his hoodie and keep him close. He doesn't know what she's dreaming about, but Tyler can bet it isn't about him. It kills him, that he can bet that.

What he wouldn't have bet on is any self-preservation left in his weary, wallowing body. Yet he does have some. Not in spades—just enough to peel his body from her sofa, which is nowhere near as comfortable (or big) as his own, though that's beside the point. Enough, for now, to run to the bathroom... to the shower, beneath its cold, unforgiving spray. Piercing him, but never more cruelly than reality.

When he gets out, his cheeks are ruddy from the cold.
It doesn't matter if it's her apartment. Grace is gone.
It kills him, that he hadn't even expected her to still be here.

He had come back to his own apartment, eventually. He couldn't even pretend he hadn't stuck around too long first. (Waiting on her. Always waiting on her, some part of him.) It didn't matter how used to her absence he'd gotten. Tyler discovers it hurts, still; a blistering pain, like slapping a sunburn.

That's what it is, to see her name light up his phone screen hours later.

GRACE: *Main St. Please come. Need you*

He could pretend to ponder, *What does she want?* The truth burns in his bones; it's the same suffocating temperature as shame. It doesn't matter what it is. He doesn't even have to ask. And it isn't even for the right reasons. His coffee has gone cold in his mug, untouched.

He nearly spills it in his haste out the door.

Here's the thing about falling in love with someone in the formative years of your life: one didn't exactly *fall* in love. Not necessarily. Sometimes, or so Tyler had once believed, people grew in love. Not just together, but around one another; weaving, not like webs, but like vines. A living thing, in-motion.

The irony of it being Grace's voice in his head when he's walking through snowy sidewalks with his boots soaked and getting achy isn't lost on him. But it's her who reminds him, *If love were enough, it would be perfect. But we don't live in a perfect world. We just don't live in one without love.* Tyler isn't a poetic man, but he'd felt poetry in those words then, by the bus stop before he'd gotten on it for the last time. Grace isn't a poetic woman—hadn't been a poetic girl, back then—so it had been twice as special. Or so he'd thought. He'd understood what she'd meant. Should that change, just because she didn't mean it anymore? Because she didn't mean it the way he did?

Tyler supposes his answer is in the fact that he shows up.

Like a fool, but a fool who keeps his word. It isn't a perfect world. It isn't one where love is enough. But it's still one where he loves her. It's one where she's standing, her hands wringing, panic-stricken. From a handful of steps away, he can hear the rising pitch of her voice. He doesn't question it before he walks up behind her.

He doesn't miss that she whips around before he reaches her. Just seeing him, her mouth flies: "It's ruined. It's all ruined. It's— Not just Harper & Co.'s. A bunch of them. It won't happen. This, all of it— I put us through this for *nothing*. It's all rui—" Tyler's mouth covers Grace's. In the dregs of a freezing November, her mouth is warm. He'll tell her it's because he saw Maggie Harper walking up the sidewalk. It isn't untrue. When he kisses her, he feels it down to toes he might lose to frostbite by the end of the evening. Grace makes a soft, wounded sound at the back of her throat, and he just knows. This is a selfish kiss; a deceptive one. A kiss that fools the elder woman, Grace, maybe even some scattered passers-by. To Tyler, it's the truest his lips have been in years, making waves over hers.

When he rears back, it's by necessity and not choice.

A sliver of air is consumed by the hot cloud of his breath, avowing, "Shh, you've come too far now, Gracie." This close, he almost goes cross-eyed, watching her bottom lip tremble. Her hands clutch at his elbows, fingernails managing to bite through all his layers in desperation.

"I don't think I can do this. I don't even know what I'm doing anymore... I bit off too much. For a client who hasn't even committed to anything." Every word is an agonized, anxious whimper.

Tyler wraps her close, lets her burrow her face in the hollow of his throat. Her ear is right there for his words to pour into the shell of, "Anyone with half a brain would know their business can only thrive with Grace Thompson attached to it. This is the moment, Gracie. She's right there. Show her who *you* are. It's cooler than the stupid foo-foo perfume and a fake boyfriend you've never needed. You don't need the frills. Just your heart."

GRACE

Your heart, Tyler tells her. Like it's that easy. She could've sworn he wasn't always this cheesy.

His pep-talk was more than she had any right to expect, regardless. She'd texted him in a moment of panic. In the midst of chaos, she'd told him she'd *needed* him—because it had felt like she did. Only a moment after she'd sent it, her nerves frayed. She'd copied the same message and sent it to Hannah, too. It felt safer, doing that. Hannah's her friend, Tyler's her friend; friends text friends for help. A + B = C.

That was before he'd kissed her.

Of course, that, too, had been in the vein of saving her from her own mouth. It hadn't felt like it, but that's not the point. She just hadn't expected it; Tyler's kiss, so different and still somehow the same. She hadn't expected her own lips to respond instinctively, though maybe, in hindsight, she should've. Or maybe she should divorce expectations altogether, for the fat load of good they aren't doing her lately. Maybe it would've hurt less when Tyler excused himself and vanished, right after she'd confessed she wanted to help all the other floats too. That Maggie's community-loving bug must've bitten her, too. She hadn't expected a high-five, but –

She doesn't expect him to bring an entire troop along with him half an hour later, either. Yet there he is. In the center of a gaggle of them—all of whom she recognizes, once she forces her eyes past the Tyler Reed of it all—leading them like they're his pack. Tyler's older than her by a fraction, and it still leaves him much younger than Ethan, Hannah and Hannah's boyfriend Noah, and Liam Brooks with the wonderful, pocket-sized Sophie.

"Um?" Grace demands from Hannah when her best friend ambles forward, bumping her freckled nose into Grace's. Behind Hannah's torrent of fiery curls, she thinks she sees a toolbox. Grace didn't think Tyler *owned* a toolbox.

"You're not as alone as you think," Hannah says, cheerfully sing-song.

Grace isn't thrilled that her eyes slip to Tyler of their own accord. She doesn't appreciate the sunny, glowing beam Hannah treats her to, too knowing, too much. "Did he—?"

Hannah's laugh is softer than usual. Somehow, all the more earnest for it. "Sure did."

He's all over the place. Like a swirling tornado, if those brought about peace instead of the opposite. *No,* Grace's exhausted brain counters, *he's like one of those Roomba vacuum cleaners. Swirling on their own, fixing, fixing, fixing.*

It hadn't been that long ago that she'd broken his heart. She's felt it, the weight of a guilt she had been sure she'd buried irretrievably, for days now. It doesn't seem real, or right, for a kiss—a hoax of a kiss, at that—to be what switched the gears in her head. It isn't fair, to anyone. After all, Tyler had been right. She did have a good head on her shoulders. She *had* had good reasons to break it off with him, no matter how much she cared about him.

But she looks at him now, his arm slung around Ethan Parker's shoulders. A grumpy-looking mechanic who doesn't seem half as fun as his ragtag gang of buddies—and Tyler makes him laugh. Makes him throw his head back and guffaw, pouring out a bark of laughter even Ethan looks shocked by. But it isn't surprising. No matter what details have shifted in Tyler's life, in his professional excellence or his social skills, in his sentimentality and his quotient of sass, this is still the same. If Grace is the weight, Tyler is the insistent hands that want to share it. To help, to linger.

What if I just tell him, she can't help but yearn. *Even with all the chaos and cataclysm, he's been glue. He isn't who he was; I'm not who I was. Maybe it hurts because my stupid heart swells ten sizes at the sight of him. I can tell him.*

How, exactly, she doesn't know. But she knows she's been quiet for too long.

For the first time in forever, Grace feels adrift without a plan. She wonders what life has been offering her lately, besides Tyler. Even reconnecting with him had been an accident, a twist of fate she hadn't planned for. As she walks down the freshly cleared street, she can't help but notice a new spring in her step, a lightness she hadn't felt in years.

Her eyes search for Tyler, and she doesn't make a secret of it.

When she finds him, though—his voice is pitched low, rough, ragged. "She really sent her the same text?" The sound that leaves him sounds closer to a groan than a laugh. It's an ugly sound. Grace feels it like an icicle plunged into her chest. "She's a robot. I don't know what I was thinking, man. She doesn't care. She can do that. She can – I'm in a box. And I get to stay there until she can use me. When she needs me. *If.* But she doesn't want me."

Grace steps back so quickly, she nearly slips. The bare brick of the wall she catches herself on leaves her palms raw. *Good,* she thinks. *Fine.* She clutches the wall harder. Her breaths try to go haywire. Grace refuses them the discrepancy, the—the weakness. She won't wear it. She won't.

"Grace!" Maggie's exclamation is bright. Vibrant. *Warm.* "You've won me over. I just had to find you and tell you. I had my doubts, you know that. I'm very protective of my business! But you... You, lady, you have been spectacular today. Gone above and beyond, shown up, and served your community with your whole heart. What a good heart, Tyler is right. Of course, I was already going to tell you that you've got the job before he found me..." As if there's a dimmer switch attached to the woman, Maggie's words taper off. Quieter.

She steps right up to Grace, her chubby fist tipping up the prideful jut of Grace's chin.

That's all it takes. It breaks inside of her like a dam she's been patching for so, so long. For the first time in years and years, Grace bursts into tears.

Chapter Six

GRACE

The broken dam dwindles to a faucet. Somehow, it's worse. It's a faucet with a broken tap, and it isn't only tears that gush. Sticky snot smears itself over her chapped cheeks, freezing there. Grace doesn't even care.

All Maggie does is smooth a hand through Grace's hair. Maggie's voice, warm and soothing, washes over Grace. Though she doesn't catch a single word, It's enough to coax the truth out of her. She says everything—divulges every bit of it, from her spiraling in the company bathroom to five minutes ago. About her insecurities and her admiration. Her fears; so many of them.

She deserves revulsion. Maybe a restraining order, since she's smudged snot over what Grace *knows* is cashmere just by feel.

Instead, the woman looks – curious. There's no censure when she asks, simply, "Why Tyler? That's sticky."

Grace's voice cracks as she tries to dismiss it all, "It doesn't matter." But Maggie's warm expression shifts, her gaze turning steely. "You lied to me, Grace," she says, her tone leaving no room for evasion. "Now, it's time for the truth."

Ludicrously, Grace wants to laugh. She'd expected someone like

Maggie Harper to be... more finessed in the art of manipulation. There was the trouble with expectations again. So, she admits, "A part of me knew he'd do it. He'd – do anything for me." The lump in her throat is painful to swallow around. Just that quickly, laughter is the last thing on Grace's mind.

"Honey," Maggie says, chuckling. Grace supposes she's earned being laughed at. "What else do you think love is?"

The undignified garbled mess that leaves her barely passes for dissent. But it's the best she has. She struggles to find the words. "It wasn't supposed to be like this. When we were together, I was terrified —always afraid he'd wake up and see what I saw: that I was taking more than I gave. I felt like a burden, a robot who couldn't return what he offered. I thought letting him go would make his life easier."

The look on Maggie's face is careful. "Why would he think that of you, Grace?" she questions, contemplative. "The girl I see in front of me is all turmoil and agony. Robots don't work that way. Not yet, at least, I don't think. But love doesn't work an even 50-50 one hundred percent of the time, either. That's not real. People make mistakes. You learn better, then make better mistakes. Love *can* hurt; anything that matters does. The right person is the one who'll tell you the truth, no matter what, and deal with it with you. Do you think he's that man for you?"

Grace doesn't say anything. She doesn't have to. It's all over her face.

"So let him be. Try to be that person back for him, if he's worth it to you. You're never doing someone favors by being less of yourself. Don't kid yourself here; if you're hiding, you're doing it for your sake. Just ask yourself: What can you do for both of yours?" Maggie pets her knee firmly, then rises to her feet.

It's long after Maggie's gone, and others have walked over the footsteps she'd tracked across the pavement, that Grace realizes she doesn't know whether or not she has the job. The job she'd done all of this for. *Lied,* and dragged a friend into – who isn't just her friend. It sinks into her like teeth, the truth: There's only one part in all of it that matters to her. It's him.

TYLER

This room is full of love. Brimming with it. But Tyler is in a bubble; insular in the worst way. It isn't Christmas yet, but he feels like a ghost haunting the occasion. Transfixed by the glow of it all; it radiates from all of them, this house that's a home and these people who are family to each other. They don't deem it *Friendsgiving*. Tyler's privy to the truth.

It should matter that he's privy to the reason Noah keeps shooting Ethan sly grins, and Liam hasn't let go of Sophie's hand since they'd sat down at the table. He can't even look too deeply at why Alex can't seem to peel his eyes away from the buxom brunette Noah had introduced as his little sister, Emily.

All he can think is, stupidly: *She doesn't need me. She just needed someone.*

He can't stop looking at her. At Grace. Looking at her like maybe, if he looks hard enough, he'll understand her. Or maybe, just maybe, he can talk himself into hating something about her. Conjure up some way to resent the way the candles cast a halo her skin siphons. To silence the persistent itch in his fickle fingertips, wanting to reach across the table and take her hand—seize it—and demand her attention. Her *consideration,* for once.

She doesn't even look back. Like she can't bear it, she doesn't even lift her head.

Tyler's never thought of himself as a tempestuous person. He'd venture he's the opposite. But every passing second she evades his searching gaze, when he's a fool, still a fool over her, still trying to understand her... A storm brews beneath his skin.

It takes a shameful amount of effort to focus on Ethan when he stands. The tall, dark brunette beside him drops her fork unceremoniously with a clatter that cuts right through the noise. Everyone goes silent. "Livvy," Ethan says, a small smile playing with the corners of his lips, his fingers scratching over his beard. "I thought a lot about how I'd do this. I've been thinking about it for a while now. You've always talked to me about how lonely you felt, growing up. Over the last year, we've spent so much time talking about—"

"Parker, oh my God—"

Ethan huffs; half-exasperated, half-enamored. "Let me *finish*, woman. I practiced this."

"Okay, but—"

"—I swear, if you try to propose first, Olivia Wright..."

Like a flip of a trigger switch, she's on her feet. They stand so close, their noses bump. She grins at him with all of her teeth; it's a feral, wild smile. Ethan stills. "No, I've got you beat. I'm pregnant. So, yeah, I'll marry you and whatever, but it'll have to be a shotgun wedding. If that's alright with you."

This time, at least it's water Liam chokes on. It's literal and visible. All Tyler chokes on is want. He wants it so bad. The rock-solid relationship. The family. Except he's only wanted it with one girl. Not only does she not want him, she won't even look at him.

All around them, loved ones begin to clink their glasses with their utensils A tradition, albeit premature, signal for the happy couple. At least until Olivia snaps, "*Oy!* That's my Grams' fancy crystal. Don't shatter it. We'll kiss when we want to kiss!" Before, of course, she yanks her groom-to-be in with a fistful of his collar.

A second, and he has to look away. He can't take it anymore. Tyler lurches to his feet. With his palms planted on the tabletop, he summons the dregs of his courage and conviction, and pours it all into the syllables of her name. "*Grace.* Talk a walk with me." He doesn't let it be a question. There's no way around it: he doesn't trust her to give him the answer he needs. As it is, she doesn't really give him an answer at all. With a wobbly jerk of her head, she stands too. Then walks out ahead of him, shaking her head to herself.

Tyler hates that it makes him worry for her. That he still can't help it.

Amidst all the joy and humor, he doubts anyone will notice them slipping out. And if he doesn't say this now, he might never. If he has to lose her, then he'll lose her. But this half-lived love won't do. Tyler *can't* do it. He can't keep waiting on the next time she foils herself into some harebrained scheme to which he's the current solution. He can take a lot, but maybe he doesn't want to. Maybe that's enough. It *would* be enough, and he would *care,* if the tables were turned. Maybe that's what he'll tell her. Maybe that's what—

Her grip on his forearm is a shock. It's stronger than he remembers it being. She jerks him to a stop forcefully, and Tyler nearly falls flat on his face. Not with a gun to his head could he guess what's about to come out of her mouth—but his chest shudders from an avalanche inside of him when she says, "I'm not a robot. I hate you for saying I am, but I hate *me* even more for almost letting you believe it. You shouldn't. I don't want you to believe that. Because I'm—in love with you, Ty. I'm *still* in love with you. I loved you then, and I love you now, and I don't know that it's enough–I want it to be, but I don't know. I *know* that you make the chaos in my head go quiet. I *know* that being a team with you is the only time I let a whole breath go. I've given you no reason to believe me. But believe me anyway."

"I love you," Tyler says dumbly. His face is numb, he thinks.

Grace means to exhale, but what comes out of her mouth is a cry. Muffled and relieved. "I know! I know you do. I've never had to guess that one for a second. I just have such a hard time believing that I deserve it. I'm so... hard, and you're so soft, Tyler. You're good and kind. And I'm going to take you for granted. And I'm so scared of what'll be the straw that breaks the camel's back."

His mouth sprawls into a grin that threatens to split his face in two. "Did you just call me a camel, Gracie?"

Grace tears up at the sight of his smile, and he reels her in. His lips press to her feathering hairline, and Tyler chides, "Lying, eavesdropping —what's next, grand theft auto?" He kisses the tip of her cold nose. "I wouldn't have you any other way. I love you when you can't see anything but the work you're so passionate about, and I love you when you relax into sleep—the way you somehow go from talking to snoring the next second. The only version of you that I can't *stand* is one I can't call mine. The one that won't look at me. And I'm so tired of pretending otherwise, just to keep you in my life in some way."

Her grip on him hasn't fallen away. If anything, she grips him tighter. "I'm so, so sorry. I want that. I do. I want to be yours. I want it —as long as you'll have me."

Tyler's smile doesn't drop entirely. But it turns a muted shade. He asks, "You're aware it's forever, aren't you?"

Like she's tired of waiting, she mutters, impatient as her hands, "It better be."

She catches his mouth in a feverish kiss that he's been tasting for years.

Chapter Seven

THE TOWN IS an autumnal delight with the volume turned up.

When the parade starts, it's as if the snowstorm was a bad dream. Now, all that permeates the crisp fall air is the spectacular warmth of roasted chestnuts and sour-sweet zinging cider. Wherever the eye wanders, the reason for the season shines. Pumpkins and cornucopias, maple leaves in greens and oranges and browns, real and paper alike. There isn't a tree on either side of the street that doesn't wink merrily with fairy lights.

It's clear which float is the most intricate, though. David Harper had already asked Grace Thompson if she thought it could be seen on Google Earth. He, and his discerning, complicated, wonderful wife, had invited Grace and her very real boyfriend, Tyler, onto the float, however. Grace can't be too peeved about them teasing her. The truth came with a price. Whatever else her very many faults, she'd never been bad at paying her dues.

Through all the teasing, and the laughter Tyler staunches in the fuzzy shoulder of his thick coat, she doesn't cow. She takes it with sheepish laughter and her ever-proud chin through every joke. When it splinters, Maggie Harper leans in, right in the middle of the parade route, to share, "You still have the job, by the way. But you're fired if you ever lie to me again. So, no fake weddings or babies, okay?"

It's a good thing Tyler reels her back against his chest. Grace suspects a feather could have knocked her over, just then. Her boyfriend helps as much as he doesn't, pressing a kiss to the crown of her head before he tugs his stupid beanie off his own head and onto hers. She giggles, and looks once more like the girl whose photo flashes on his phone's screen every time she calls him.

As the town is a chaotic chorus of joy around them, Grace tips her head back and asks Tyler, "How about real ones someday soon?"

The End

Sweet Secret

Chapter One

ALEX

Being a single man in his 30s isn't something Alex Carter dwells on often.

It's easy enough to evade when it comes up in conversation. All it takes is a wry remark like, *I'm a teacher. Do you know what we make?* His current success rate for getting out of blind date set-ups is through the roof.

That makes it all the more humbling when he finds himself grateful for the round table shape that takes up most of Ethan and Olivia's dining room. He sets down the dish of reheated turkey casserole. The majority of his social circle in his little small town populates the rest of the table. All of them are in pairs. Just like the missing two, with Tyler having carted Grace all the way to New Jersey to spend two weeks with his parents.

Closest to him sit his friends Sophie Davis and Liam Brooks. It may have been Liam who he's known longer—having been a staple in his life almost as long as his cousin, Ethan has—but it's Sophie that Alex is closer to. Probably because Sophie isn't as abrasive; it's effortless to feel close to her. Not unlike the apple-cheeked redhead beside her, Hannah Baker, who currently shows Sophie something on some Pinterest board.

Her other hand is twined with Noah Harrison's on top of the table. Noah's refereeing an argument between Ethan's fiancée, Liv, and Liam. He plays with the rings stacked on Hannah's fingers. The only one still missing from the table is Ethan. But he'd offered to grill, intent on keeping Liv off her feet no matter how early in the stages of her pregnancy she is.

Alex watches.

He isn't typically the idling spectator of the group. That's his cousin. Sophie sometimes calls Alex a 'pot-stirrer in cahoots;' something Alex takes no offense to, given the person he's usually *in cahoots* with is her boyfriend. She doesn't mind it either, he's sure. Liam may be abrasive on a good day, but there's no discounting the tenderness of the way he plays with the ends of Sophie's hair now. The girl who uses phrases like 'in cahoots.' They fit. Differently, but no less than Hannah and Noah do; having known each other all their lives, since their sandbox days, just like Liam and Ethan, only to grow up and fall in love one serendipitous fall.

"Don't start without me," Ethan's gruff voice warns from the patio.

Olivia grins devilishly. "Even me?" she sing-songs back.

There's a pause. She's laughing before Ethan replies. Then again, his fiancée isn't the only one who knows exactly what Ethan, who comes to lean in the doorway, will say: "You're the exception to everything, Mrs. Parker." They aren't going to be wed for another month or so. It doesn't stop Liv from beaming ecstatically. She doesn't correct him.

Alex can tell: they fit, too. Even one who couldn't see would feel it. It's more a myth than anything, now, that they'd once butted heads constantly.

All of them are like puzzle pieces, slotted together. Alex doesn't know what that makes him. He doesn't want to think about it too much. Could it just be the literary aficionado in him that's grasping at motifs and metaphors? Possibly. He'd swear he doesn't get so lost in his head *every* week. There's evidence of it.

After all, the bunch of them do this every Sunday, getting together to break bread around one of their tables. The location is always chosen in sporadic rotation ruled by nothing but the host's convenience. (Occasionally, by a competitive, best-out-of-three game of Rock, Paper, Scissors—but that's neither here nor there.)

Maybe it's just that it's Ethan and Olivia's table they're at again.

Alex doesn't have to think too hard to place the last time he was here. Not that he's got anything against his cousin, his cousin's girl, or their house. The house itself is technically new to all of them. Olivia, too. But neither feel it. It's the house Olivia Wright's late grandmother had left her when she'd passed away the year before. The couple had been together almost since Liv had moved to town; they'd been living together for most of it, unofficially. It's a homey place. All the more so when every room of it is filled with laughter and sass. Alex likes it. It's cozy, with or without the fire that burns in the hearth now. A different kind of warmth than his own fixer-upper of a two-bedroom, populated with several cats, but a comforting one all the same.

His problem—and it is, in fact, a *problem*—is with something else, entirely. Some*one* else. Himself. And it's all—

"—Emily's heading it?" Alex hadn't thought he'd tuned out. But it becomes awfully clear he did the moment he tunes back in. His attention snaps like an elastic band, pulled too taut, breaking. It falls from Sophie's lips, and Alex nearly falls out of his chair. With what—*shock?* Eagerness? He doesn't want to think about it. He shouldn't be thinking about it. He has zero right to. Less than zero right to!

He has no control over it, his unfairly facetious inner critic mocks.

He doesn't have to accept it to know: his brain has been trying to busy itself all evening, and his eyes making a concentrated effort not to linger on Noah. Noah is one of his closest friends in the world. Somehow, Alex doubts his mooning over the *little sister* of one of his closest friends in the world will go well. He doesn't plan to find out, either way.

He's been familiar with Emily Harrison's face since he was eighteen years old. Never, in all those years, up till Thanksgiving two weeks ago, has it *haunted* Alex like this. She'd once had the same straw-colored hair Noah does, that fell in a silky waterfall down her back and now doesn't. Now, her hair is dark; not dark, chestnut brown like Olivia's or raven black like Liam's, but a rich, confounding marriage of dark and milk chocolate. A color so beautiful, it demands descriptors belonging to dessert. Her laughter, that's sweet as marshmallows, and her voice smoky as a campfire.

Subtle.

Clearing his throat, Alex stands. "I'm gonna see if Ethan needs an extra pair of hands."

His mouth forgets the memo less than an hour later. It's apropos of nothing that he turns to Sophie's bubbly blonde head, and blurts: "So, what were you talking about earlier? Um. Emily– Noah's sister's heading something?" He tries for casual, but suspects he progresses right past its purview.

Sophie doesn't even blink twice. She turns away from the fire where she'd been warming her freshly washed hands, nodding exuberantly. "The Snowball Charity Fundraiser!" she exclaims. "A mouthful, I know, but it's for an amazing cause. It's—well, another mouthful, so bear with me. *But!* Low-income families with chronic health conditions. If you looked at the numbers, it'd blow your socks off, Alex. And it's going to be a *black-tie* affair. It was Em's idea, obviously, and she's so nice. Genuinely, *so* nice. But hey, you know that. Duh. You knew her as a kid, right? I forget sometimes that you've all known each other forever. Probably as often as I forget I *haven't* known you all forev—"

"Soph, *breathe,*" Liv insists, poking Sophie's hip with a socked toe from her armchair.

All Alex can do is hope it's distraction enough to cover the way his breath shallows. It had been his own fault. Still, he squirms. He's never felt more obvious in his life, and there seems to be little he can do about it. The only saving grace is Sophie's sanguine nature. She cares with every inch of her heart, wildly, incessantly. It doesn't occur to her that Alex may have ulterior motives behind the random inquiry. So Alex evades Olivia's obtrusive gaze instead.

He has to, when words bubble out of his mouth: "That does sound amazing, Soph. Can I... help out?" His brain gives him a two-second warning. His mouth has already decided it's a fantastic idea. His heart pounds furiously in his chest, helpless to stop any of it.

Sophie beams with unfettered excitement. "Oh, Emily will be *thrilled,* Alex, wow."

Good job. Now you can't get out of it if you want to!

He doesn't even see Liam approach. He'd been sampling whatever decadent concoction it was that Hannah had brought along for dessert, last Alex had checked. "Dude, do you even have time with school?" His voice startles from behind. It's Liam's hand catching on his arm that keeps him from tripping into the hearth.

Panic permeates his tenor. "*Sure!*" It comes out too high in pitch. Suspicious—or whatever is ten paces ahead of it. "I always have time for community. All part of shaping the young minds of tomorrow, man. You know. Be the change you want to see in the world... et cetera."

He hears Olivia snort and pointedly refuses to look at her.

EMILY

Inside the immaculate, sleek black folder, past the spreadsheets rife with facts and figures, is a vision board. There's nothing professional about it. It's an accumulation of photographs, fabrics, and color palette swatches. Amidst the rest of the organization, it's a moment of chaos. Emily Harrison runs her fingertips over it gently, thoughtfully. The edges of the haphazardly glued pieces scrape deliciously. There's whimsy to it.

Whimsy doesn't have a choice but to draw a sharp contrast in this room. Amongst the dark and regal furnishings of her father's study, even Emily is one more prop. Dressed in a navy, matching pajama set, she paints as somber a picture as anything else in here. This isn't an accident. It's a choice. Emily's made so many choices, lately—but this one, arguably the most important one to the trajectory of her life, isn't hers to make. It's only hers to pitch for.

It hadn't always been this way. Maybe that's why, even now, she isn't uncomfortable in this room. She never had been. It had been effortless for the little girl she'd been to sneak through the hallowed halls of this house too far past her bedtime and steal away into this room. It smells like her father's preferred brand of cigars and leather. She rarely ever got caught. When she did, it was by her father, sitting in the chair she can fill out herself now; he'd always scooted the chair back and let her sit in his lap. His smooth, low voice explaining whatever paperwork was laid out in front of him to her had always been sweeter than any lullaby.

Alone in here, Emily sits alert. Her nerves, a little frayed. The pressure almost crushing.

"Emily? Sweetheart, it's late," sounds from the doorway. It's only her mom. To most anyone, Vivian Harrison wouldn't cut such an imposing figure. She's a slight woman; her figure not as full as Emily's, even in her sixties. Her hair is a darker, more regal blonde than what Emily had halfway inherited from her—not that Emily's recent dye job exposes it. There's no real reason for the way her palms moisten with nervous sweat. That may be what's most disconcerting about it.

Still, she forces her voice to steadiness. Her hands, too, when they inconspicuously flip to a different page in the folder. "Hi, mama," Emily says softly. "I know it is. I was just—"

"Working?" her mother offers. Her smile is exhausted, but not unkind. Emily knows she doesn't mean it acrimoniously. Her mother isn't a snide woman. She's just one who is confounded by her daughter's choices. Between the both of them, Emily doesn't know which one of them has molded that distance into a barrier. She only knows the barrier has become impermeable. A fact that is undeniable when they are facing one another, under the same roof, instead of over the phone.

Sheepishly, Emily nods her agreeance. "Just a little. But I'm not *up* because I'm working. The opposite, maybe. It's weird being back home." Her shrug feels clumsy and too young, two things she makes a concentrated effort not to be these days.

For a moment, her mother is quiet. Her eyes, the same intriguing blue-green both of Emily's brothers share, appraise Emily carefully. She hates that it unnerves her. She hates the way tension needles beneath her breastbone, wondering if her mother will admonish her. It's her *home*. It's the last place on earth that should feel strange to be. All true, and Emily knows it. Yet, while she's working herself up into a tizzy, all her mother says is, "Well, try some warm milk, sweetheart. Don't be up too late, okay?" Every word is soft. Measured. Everything Emily isn't, on purpose.

"I won't," Emily says quickly. "I'll try it. Thank you. I, uh- Love you."

Her mother looks at her for a beat. How such a soft gaze can pierce her so totally, Emily can't fathom. She is skewered, regardless. "I love you, too," Vivian Harrison ultimately says, before she's gone as soundlessly as she'd come. She leaves behind a heavy silence, one that settles on Emily's chest; a reminder of the moment when she'd shouted at her mother: *I love you, but I don't want to be you!*

Choices aren't always voluntary, and their aftermath lasts regardless. She doesn't have to wonder about it to know, in her very bones, that if her mother's the one who erected the barrier, then it isn't like Emily never gave her reason to erect it.

Sleep, in Emily's experience, doesn't fix everything. But it does help. Not a remedy; it is at least a balm. The persistent, drilling headache she'd come to bed with is dulled when the winter sun spills in through the still-open, dusty rose drapes in her childhood bedroom.

It only takes her a single, fortifying, *deep* breath to pluck her phone from the bedside table. She doesn't realize her shoulders have stiffened until she feels them uncoil at the name on the screen. She swipes to see Sophie has starter a group chat with her and Alex.

> Sophie: EM!!! I'm SO pleased to tell you Alex here volunteered himself to be of assistance with event prep! He's good with everything from sweet-talking people to manly lifting tasks! Yay! We're the 3 Musketeers now btw. Philanthropy style.

For reasons unbeknownst to her, her heart pitter-patters inside her chest. Her cheeks burn. But there's no one around to see it, so Emily leaves it be. For the teenager that she'd once been, who'd sported heart-eyes for her brother's friend for years. Long enough ago, but not so long that she can't blame muscle memory when her face flushes the way it used to every time Alex Carter walked into a room, as she messages him now.

> Emily: Should we come up with an official title for you?

> Alex: Errand Boy?

> Emily: Beck & Call Boy? Man?

> Alex: Personal Assistant?

> Emily: Now that's just unimaginative, Mr. Carter

Alex: Ew, just Alex is fine, Em.

Emily: You're not even going to try to call me Ms. Harrison?

Alex: I could if that's one of the beck's you're calling. But it's pretty close to what I call your mom...

Emily: Point taken. Want to grab dinner tomorrow? We can iron out some details. Catch up. I barely got to talk to you at Thanksgiving!

Ironically, a teenager is precisely what she feels reduced to when he doesn't reply as swiftly as they'd been pinging back and forth. The silence gnaws. Emily reminds herself, forcefully: *You're an adult. Act like it. Move on.* But she knows, as she rolls out of bed and washes her face. She's an adult, with an in-depth morning skincare routine. She has nutrition goals to hit with breakfast. One could even say she has no time in her schedule to fret about a boy—*man?*—to text (or not text, apparently) her back.

She still nearly spills milk on the immaculate kitchen floor when her cellphone buzzes with a notification an hour and a half later.

Alex: Sorry, had to take a class. Is tonight too soon, Emily? Just name the time and place. We'll make it happen.

No one can see the look that sprawls across her face. So, she adamantly decides it simply does not have to count.

Chapter Two

EMILY

Call her old-fashioned, but Emily had been raised to know it's respectful to dress up for someone. She shows up early, on purpose. Polished in a short plaid wool skirt over thick tights, and a deep maroon V-neck sweater that settles prettily over her collarbones. Former object of her adolescent affections or not, she still would've taken care in putting herself together for anyone she was meeting for a meal.

She maintains that the whole way across town to the diner she'd chosen for them to meet.

The fact that it's a meager walk from the local high school isn't why she's chosen it. Emily had genuinely missed *Loretta's*. While in the city, it's what she'd missed most often. In the wake of a taxing day, or a casual heartache, sometimes a girl just wants a hamburger. No one makes 'em quite like Loretta Beam. It isn't like Emily hadn't gone looking.

Sat at the counter with her winter-bitten fingertips warming against the hot ceramic of her mug, she stares into the depths of her tea like there are answers in the leaves to be decoded. It's fine. It isn't the future that's on Emily's mind anyway.

Almost as if she were under a spell, the past lures her attention and holds it arrested. In some ways, it's Maplewood Grove's fault. No matter

how much things change, this town, with all its loveliness and aggrava-
tions, remains the same. She sits at the counter of the diner, watching
Loretta chatter to the town's sheriff, Colton Rhodes, and thinks of how
Loretta used to tease Emily.

Back when she'd been a slip of a girl with dark blonde hair, who
hadn't yet grown into her features and blushed furiously at every
sighting of the first boy (to whom she wasn't related) who'd ever been
nice to her and called her pretty. It had felt like a revelation every time
their paths had crossed, back then. The sheer intensity of emotions that
she could feel without any potential for it to be requited.

That isn't who she is nowadays.

Emily has spent years building a life of balance and self-assurance.
Respect—it's a non-negotiable, and she demands it in every interaction.
Confident in who she's become, she's no longer the awkward girl who
once envied her older brother Noah's poise. Now, she's the one others
look to—strategic, assertive, and sometimes even daring.

So why is it that, as the diner's glass door swings open at a grown-up
Alex Carter's behest, her stomach somersaults over the sight of him? She
doesn't lose herself in it. Her features remain composed; cool, and
collected. There's a resting, idle smile on his chapped lips. As if he just
walks around, content to exist. There are lines to his face that hadn't
been there all those years ago, of course. The crow's feet around eyes that
have always overtaken the rest of his features; the specific, deep color of
melted chocolate. Laugh lines edged around his mouth, which isn't so
sprawled that the single dimple she recalls in his left cheek might flash.
But they enhance that *Alex* essence. There's no detraction.

When those warm eyes land on her, she manages to keep her breath
from hitching. Her chest tightens. But there is no missing the way his
face splits open with raw astonishment. Suddenly, Emily doesn't care
how undeniably her pleasure at this shines through.

She likes what she sees in his face when he walks up. She doesn't
know what it is, specifically, that she feels she's won. She only knows it
feels like she's won *something*.

His eyes haven't left her. Then again, he's hardly sat staring at her in stunned silence, either. Had Emily gotten the chance to dwell on it, it may have been her wearing the astonishment next. But she doesn't get that chance.

Once her heart is done going haywire at the sweet kiss he presses to her cheek, one-armed hugging her hello, they get to talking. And once they start, it doesn't let up. It's organic and effortless. Like they've been doing it for years. Time flies.

"This girl *really* said the words, 'I don't like reading,' and I swear I just stared at her for a solid three minutes," Alex is saying, his face halfway buried in his palm.

Emily huffs with affront. "What does that even *mean?* That kind of blanket statement, like—there are so many genres out there! There's *audio*books. Those count. You're not one of those snobs who think it doesn't count, are you?"

"Of course not." Alex shakes his head quickly, but not defensively. Emily giggles. "It counts. I feel like we, as a society, need to move past that narrow-minded narrative. It's about absorbing stories, period. Building empathy, exploring themes and characteristics through litera-ture, and building those analytical skills. So, to hear someone just baldly claim that reading is just..."

Emily sucks down an emphatic slurp of her hot chocolate. "And you're an *English teacher!* I don't know if that makes me presumptuous because obviously not every English teacher has to be a bookworm – but come on. Know your audience, right?"

"Right!" He points with a french fry, and she doesn't think twice before leaning across the table to bite off a chunk. She just narrowly misses his fingers. Emily relishes the way it's his face that floods with color. If she'd felt like a shrinking violet by the counter, she feels like a willow tree now. Nevertheless, he recovers quickly. He doesn't blink before popping the rest of the fry in his own mouth and adding, "So, now that I've talked your ear off about my exciting career as a high school English teacher... Why don't you tell me more about what you're doing back in town with this fundraiser?"

Emily's mouth scrunches up a little at that. "Why would you put down your job? I really admire what you do, Alex. In fact, I think you're criminally underpaid for it. That's not your job being small; it's society having bizarre priorities."

"Oh, I didn't—" he fumbles. She can't believe she makes him fumble. Just like that, she's fighting a smile all over again. Alex doesn't make it easy for her. He's so earnest when he says, "I was just joking. I don't... I love my job. I chose it for a reason. But it isn't exciting. A lot of the time, it's actually pretty frustrating. Sometimes, at the end of a long day, it feels like my life is small. I've never had that *thing*, you know? That ambition that Noah and Liam have. That *you* have. I'm not hungry for anything that way. I've got my quiet life with chaos that kicks up twice a year for school plays, and that's it. And I like it. It isn't glamorous, though. I don't see the point in pretending otherwise."

While he talks, Emily finds herself nodding along. Absorbing what he says. Listening, carefully—because, while Alex talks a lot, she gets the feeling he does most of that talking to make other people feel comfortable. Emily's never been uncomfortable with silences. If anything, it's an absence of them that usually leaves her squirming and overstimulated. It's why there isn't a shadow of reluctance when she counters: "Glamour is overrated. Trust me, I've just spent years in New York. And all anyone needs at the end of the day, and I *really* believe this, is to feel seen. To belong. To have some sort of purpose. From what I'm hearing? You check all of those boxes. You don't need to hunger when you're just... sated." She knows, without having to think about it, that it's the most honest thing she's said to anyone in years. Maybe ever.

Alex looks at her wordlessly. She isn't sure he doesn't move in slow motion—and maybe it's just the way she can't tear her eyes away from him, either—as his mouth curves softly, so sweetly, at her spiel. "How could anyone not see you, Emily Harrison?"

ALEX

There may have been a slight error in his judgment.

What had he been thinking? The truth is, Alex isn't sure he was thinking at all. He'd convinced himself it was harmless to message Emily back. A little back and forth; did it really matter how rapid-fire the pace, or that he'd found himself replying underneath his desk while his students took a quiz? It hadn't felt like a big deal. Just like it hadn't felt like a big deal when he'd run all the way from school to his house just to change his shirt (*...twice*), or when he'd had to lean into a hug when breathing in Emily's sweet-spicy perfume had made him a little light-headed. After he'd recovered—pretty swiftly and, if he could say so himself, admirably—the conversation had flowed seamlessly. No awkwardness to be found! No different, Alex had thought, than hanging out with one of the guys.

Last he'd checked, though, none of the guys made him squirm. Flustered, with his face on fire. Forget the guys, he hadn't felt this distressed when he'd walked in on Ethan and Olivia canoodling on their patio a few weeks ago!

If Alex didn't know any better (and he isn't sure he does, come to think of it) he'd say Emily is enjoying his distress. Her pretty hazel eyes are bright as Christmas lights while she watches him. He could have sworn he saw her breath hitch over his words. Or maybe he's just another victim of wishful thinking. Her features smooth over too quickly for him to be able to read into them. A mercy, or a curse, Alex can't be sure.

Definitely not as sure as she comes off, asking, so matter-of-fact: "So, what do you see?"

Her voice is so soft. It's almost husky. He's too aware of the way she leans in close. Alex had never thought the tables scattered around *Loretta's* to be particularly small, not even the two-chaired ones like the one he and Emily occupy. But it feels it, now. Small. Too small to resist temptation without it being a mean feat. He's not aware enough, that there should be no temptation at all. His eyes shouldn't be drifting to her full mouth, stained in a nude lipstick that, somehow, only accentuates it. He shouldn't still be feeling the scrape of her teeth against the pad of his finger.

He tries to push past it. Alex tries to speak—to say something, say *anything*—but all that leaves him is a strangled exhale. Some kind of incoherent sound. *What does he see?* A gorgeous, compassionate, clever, and funny woman. "My boss," Alex huffs, finally. As if his own words are a buoy he's spotted while adrift amidst choppy waters, he grasps at it with unambivalent desperation. "How about— After we're done eating, 'course— why don't you show me the venue? Since I'm going to be helping out, it makes sense to, uh... scope. Yeah. Scope things out." He nods, afterward, like he's cementing the words into place.

Surely, this is the right call. Emily expels another bright flash of laughter and agrees gamely. She isn't offended. She even seems genuinely enthusiastic about it. "Have you ever seen the old Windham estate on the edge of town?" she asks. "It's beautiful. Totally unused. I've been talking to Dot. She's been an extraordinary help, getting the right permits into place for it. Technically, it isn't a landmark yet. And we've gotten permission to use it for the event. It's for a beautiful cause, but I still wasn't sure it would all come through for a minute there. Its aura is just..." Emily sighs, tapering off. Alex doesn't think he's ever heard a sigh sound giddy before, yet she manages. Contradicting its softness, her palms slap down on the table a second later. "You know what? I'm done eating. Are you done eating? Let's go see it. I've got the keys on me all the time."

Her enthusiasm is a tide that he can't help but get swept up in. Alex strives to match it, shoving away from the table and onto his feet. "Let's do it," he practically cheers. There's no time to be embarrassed about it. Emily doesn't even blink before she rushes to the register. Before he can even think about protesting, she's already paid Loretta and is leaning across the countertop to press a kiss to the woman's cheek. She's been away a little over six years, and she still looks at home. Alex is taken aback by it.

He's taken aback by a lot about Emily Harrison, as it turns out.

He grapples, belatedly protesting when she returns to him, "I was going to—" Emily waves him off, literally, and the gesture reminds him so much of her brother that he has no choice but to fall silent. Which, Alex admits, may be the right option. She says herself, shrugging into a black trench coat that looks like it's worth more than his entire paycheck, "Business expense," because it isn't like this was a date. Sure, none of his other colleagues had ever bitten his finger... but maybe that's just because he works in a school.

Alex doesn't know. He doesn't know anything when she hooks her arm through his and tugs him out the door. On a cerebral level, he understands that they have known each other for most of their lives. But, really, they've known *of* each other. One summer, years ago, back when he'd been nineteen and getting to know his cousin's fancy room-mate from Columbia, he'd run into his little sister in the Harrisons' gargantuan kitchen. That young girl, with her blotchy face and knobby knees, didn't remotely resemble this iteration of herself. Every cell in his body zings with recognition, even as he grapples with how brand new, and novel, and irresistibly interesting this Emily is.

"Did you bring a car?" Alex asks her, trying to shake off the hypnosis of her proximity.

Emily hums, and it vibrates somewhere in the depths of her throat. "No. I could call for one, but... I kind of want to walk, if that's okay with you. I – missed this. Winter in Maplewood Grove." He doesn't refute it. He doesn't want to. Just walking beside her, ensconced in Emily's warm disposition and warmer charm, it's easy to grant December's bite absolution, after all.

In hindsight, it isn't very surprising at all that his strategy backfires. Maybe he really has been single for too long. It's made him exceptionally obtuse when it comes to his own lures. Alex totally feels at fault, not foreseeing that seeing a strong, magnetic woman in her element would be enticing. It doesn't matter, that this has never been an irresistible characteristic to him before. Watching Emily, listening to her, as she walks through the imposing mansion with its ornate moldings and pillars, painting a picture for Alex's mind with her vision... He doesn't understand how anyone could not be enticed.

There's zeal to her. And strategy to her pitch. Mostly, she's got heart. A passion burns in her eyes; a creative spark alight in her, building towards tangible, breathtaking fire. She's impressive and carries it like chips on both of her shoulders. It can't be a risk to put his own time and energy into this project. Her vision brooks no arguments. This fundraiser *will* be a success.

"How can I help?" Alex asks. He isn't ashamed of the undiluted sincerity of the words.

How can he be anything but glad, when she lights up like this? Happy, like a kid on Christmas morning. He doesn't have a present for her. Alex doubts he could ever come up with one for her she would actually need. Still, he'd give her anything he could. It *is* generous what she's doing.

She's just also terribly attractive. Especially when she pulls a notepad out of her tiny purse, and decides: "Time for a task list."

Chapter Three

ALEX

Somehow, once his feet get moving, Alex winds up at *E&O Auto*. The auto shop is co-owned by his cousin and his fiancée, one of which Noah had been an investor before the two merged their workshops earlier this year. Liam had poured endless time and expertise into building the new establishment. Alex can't deny that he winds up in the office in the corner too often.

He'd grown up with two older sisters, Ava and Alice. Ethan Parker was the closest thing Alex had ever had to a brother. It was rarely Alex who needed advice. His life, for the most part, was fairly formulaic. But he knows, before he ever walks through the door, that's exactly what he's in dire straits over tonight.

"Noah's serious about nothing else in life. But he's always been serious about Emily. About... boundaries, around Emily," Alex vents. Truthfully, venting to Ethan was only marginally better than doing it to a wall. It wasn't much, but Ethan had plenty of vague, sympathetic noises to give. It wasn't much, but it wasn't nothing.

He makes a half-grunt of a sound. "That's not entirely true," Ethan says.

"What are you talking about? It's completely true." Alex believes the sound that's just left him can best be described as a *squawk*.

Ethan isn't fazed. "Noah's plenty serious. He just doesn't dwell. That's not the same thing," he counters somberly. *Of course, he'll side with his best friend.* Maybe it isn't fair of his head. He can't help but think about it anyway.

"So, he's going to hate me." Alex sighs, teetering the edge of acceptance.

"Noah's never hated a single person."

"So, I'll be the first? I don't know how I feel about this world record, man..." It isn't attractive, Alex knows, to be so self-pitying. He isn't, ordinarily. It's difficult not to feel overwhelmed.

Especially when Ethan pivots away from the motorcycle he's been working away at and shoots him a flat, humorless look. He shakes his head. For a paralyzing moment, Alex is convinced that's all he's going to get. And then, Ethan drawls, "You overthink. You always overthink. And it makes you a great guy a lot of the time, Alex. You're one of the most straight-up considerate dudes I know – but, man, you've got to chill. Do you... get that you're leaping 'bout 80 paces ahead of where you're actually at?" His reality check slices at Alex. Ethan isn't deterred. "How about you see if this thing has legs first? It isn't the 1950s. She isn't a teenager he's a protective brother over, and definitely one who's got a crush on you. Emily is her own person. A grown woman. Maybe you want to try getting the girl to like you back before you start flipping out about her brother's approval. Just a thought."

Alex doesn't know if he should be happy or not, that one of the guys, even if it *is* his cousin, has finally left him flustered, with his face burning, after all.

Ethan bothers to impart wisdom so rarely that when he does, it takes up space in one's mind adamantly.

Alex sleeps on it. Wakes up and puts himself together, and heads to work. He forces himself to pay attention to his lesson plans. Fortunately,

Tuesday is one of his easier days. By the time he's at the tail-end of his day, an idea flashes in his head like a tricky lightbulb.

As luck would have it, as if specifically in the vein of the most theatrical timing, right as the class ends and the students begin to rise and file out of the room, Alex exclaims: "*Wait!*" A legion of his pupils turn around. By God's grace, somehow, most of them don't look hassled by it. That bodes well, Alex thinks.

"A friend of mine," he starts, clearing his throat, "is in charge of something called a Snowball Charity Fundraiser next week. It doesn't have anything to do with snow. The name is misleading, I know. But I'm guessing 'raising money for low-income families with chronic health conditions' wouldn't be so pithy. A little depressing?" There is a smattering of laughter. Alex smiles to himself. He almost forgets sometimes, that he's actually pretty good at this job of his. "Regardless. I'm helping her out. And I know a whole bunch of you are anxiously working away on your college applications. I get it, I've been there."

"A century ago, Mr. Carter?" A spunky redhead named Abigail chirps.

Alex snorts. "Something like that," he allows. "How*ever*. I wanted to give some of you – whoever's interested in some padding before it's time for deadlines – if you'd like to be part of the team. Entertainment, catering, there are a bunch of ways to give back and help yourself out at the same time." He can see it plainly, the anxious interest that splays itself across multiple faces. He smiles warmly, gesturing broadly. "I'll leave a list up on my desk in the morning. Take today, think it over, and if you're interested, just sign yourself up."

Volunteer management had been one of the tasks Emily had entrusted him with. Immediately, he'd thought of his friends. He'd thought, *Maybe she didn't want to ask Noah herself.* But that was narrow-minded, he sees. There could be other reasons. No matter what they were, she'd put her faith in him to deal with it.

Idly, Alex wonders if this is how his kids feel, bring up an assignment to him that they've worked hard on: with a flurry of anxiety and giddy pride intermingling in their chests. He's surprised his breaths don't leave in bubbles, like the mouth of a bottle of champagne.

He's had Emily's number since Sunday. Sophie had passed it on without a second thought. When Emily had preferred to trade quips over email, he hadn't contested it. Now, it's for the first time in his life, that afternoon, that Alex actually calls her. He can only hope he doesn't meet an untimely demise before she actually answers...

EMILY

Across the street from the local high school, Emily stands leaning against an alcove in the *Whispering Willow*. The town's premier bookstore, owned by Patty Sullivan, is an eclectic, eccentric, and worldly rabbit hole. In her hands, she holds a hefty hardcover book. A vintage copy of *Peter Pan,* she's as immersed in the contents as she'd been at 10, and 15, and 20. Truth be told, it takes her a couple of minutes to even hear her phone's persistent buzzing in her purse.

Her eyes blink away the fog as she answers. "Hello?" Just as quickly, they widen to startled saucers when the voice down the line is warm and familiar, Alex Carter saying, "Hi there, boss." It's a good thing there's a book in her hands. Emily doesn't know what she'd do with her hands they were empty.

"Hi?" Emily laughs, the pitch rising at the end, almost hysterically. "Alex... Carter?"

"Do you know that many of us? Yeah. Alex Carter," he says, downright chattering. "I have an update for you. So, I thought I'd share."

Emily blinks at the wall, baffled. "Update," she echoes. She'd only delegated some tasks off her brimming plate last night. Wasn't it a Tuesday? Wasn't he at *work?* "Don't you have a job?" she asks, and it comes out sharper than she'd intended for it to. Suspicion acts as a whetstone for her syllables.

Alex's laughter is like brandy poured down the line. Warm and sweet. It sets heat blaring at the base of her throat. "I'm a man of many trades," he jokes.

"Jack," Emily corrects.

"Alex, actually," he counters. He's ridiculous.

Her lips press themselves into a flat line. Like her hands, her face doesn't know what to do with itself either. She wasn't remotely prepared for this... encounter. She *really* isn't prepared for him to say: "Why don't you come over to my place tonight? We can order some food. Talk a little more about fundraiser details. Maybe... hang out?"

At this point, Emily doesn't need to turn to the window glass to see her reflection and confirm it. Her best friend in the world, Phoebe Baker, walks up to her. Phoebe's face feels like a mirror to her own:

gaping, obviously. Somehow, Phoebe manages to pinch at her wrist, reminding her to reply. *Make words,* her best friend mouths intensely.

Emily lets loose another slightly unhinged giggle. "Sure?" she blurts. The shoe, Emily finds, isn't as satisfying on the other foot. She liked him flustered. This, she doesn't like. It is, to put it lightly, mortifying. It takes effort to manage coherent, steady words. "Send me your location. I'll... See you?"

When he hangs up, his laughter is still clouding her head.

Phoebe's voice is a needle through a hot air balloon a millisecond after. "*What... the... actual—*" With a distressed snicker, Emily covers her best friend's mouth before she can curse a blue streak, the way Phoebe is prone to do when a situation calls for it. She can't deny that this one probably takes the cake. But, still – Emily maintains a certain sanctity to some places. The *Whispering Willow* is one of the few. "Not here."

The short, rosy-cheeked girl smacks Emily's hand away, though she nods grudging acquiescence. "Since *when* are you on phone call terms with..." It wouldn't be Phoebe if she didn't pause for dramatic effect. "*Alex. Carter.*" She punctuates it with a squeal, jumping a little on the spot.

Emily doesn't even try to stop the color that paints her cheeks around Phoebe. Though she's younger than Emily by a couple of years, the two of them had grown up next door to one another all their lives. There was no season of her life Phoebe had missed, no matter how much distance Emily's pursuit of higher education had put between them. She'd barely made it to Phoebe's impromptu wedding a couple of months ago! Somehow, though, they managed to stand the test of time.

More, and better, than anyone else could ever dream of understanding, it's Phoebe who understands, retrospectively, what these burgeoning developments would have once meant to the girl Emily had been. A girl who, try as she might to erase her, still lived in the lining of Emily's skin. Maybe she always would.

"Apparently," Emily murmurs, hugging the hardback cover into her chest, "since now."

Having a crush on a scrawny, tawny-haired teenage boy wasn't much at all like a grown, toned, tawny-haired man enticing you. It's sat on the dangerously cushy couch in Alex Carter's living room, set up right in front of the fire he's got raging in the hearth, that Emily must face this. There's no choice.

But there are Chinese takeout boxes chattered across his coffee table. "I wanted you to have options," Alex had said. Now, watching her spear a piece of moo shu pork with a fork, he chuckles at her, and tells her, "I should've known you'd end up a trailblazer in hindsight. You always did say you had no patience for chopsticks. No matter what anyone else at the table was doing; even as a kid, you were game to push back."

Emily didn't know if it was that he remembered anything about her from a time she'd never expected to be noticed by him or the way he looked at her now, but she refilled her glass with the bottle of wine she'd brought. Looking at her, with firelight dancing in his eyes, they look like pools of liquid gold. "And now look at me," she giggles, taking a ginger sip of wine. There's a cat curled up by her hip, kneading its paws drowsily against her thigh. Her head is almost quiet, for a moment. "Trailblazing all over a charity fundraiser. With my own beck and call guy, even."

"That's me," Alex agrees cheerfully, popping a dumpling in his mouth. He uses chopsticks with a little too much finesse. "A bunch of my students are signing up to be volunteers. I asked, and they don't care if you put it on the press release. It's cool, doing two great things for two different communities with the same event, Em."

Despite the fog still threatening to encroach on her pragmatic mind, Emily smiles at him. "Thanks to you," she commends. "It's an awesome idea. Honestly, thank you. I also saw that you have technical support covered. The inimitable Sophie Davis has already blessed us with catering and decor contacts. The silent auction is a go. We just have to finalize something for entertainment."

Alex offers, almost entirely seriously, "Want me to hop on stage with a mic and a book of poetry? Slam poets are still a thing."

"Depends," Emily quips.

"On?"

"Is it your book of poetry?" She doesn't understand why that makes him squirm. Not after everything he'd said about his feelings about his own life. As gently as she can, she prompts, "You're very jobful. You do all kinds of them. Just... not the one you used to want. You wanted to be a writer, remember? The next great American novel?"

"Jobful isn't a word, Emily." She can't tell, for sure. But Alex's smile manages to look somber. "I guess I realized I didn't have anything interesting to say." Emily doesn't know whether she ought to be pleased by the alarm she incites, scoffing as she does. It isn't a derisive sound; it just isn't a friendly one either. She steals a dumpling from him, chewing thoughtfully. The words feel fragile. She only wants to handle them with care. "I don't believe that. I see you, you know. You're a sponge. You absorb everything around you. I just don't buy that you've got nothing to say."

She doesn't actually expect an answer from him. In fact, she suspects what will happen next—and it's what does. Alex grins a self-conscious grin. Then segues. How can she not fall for it, though? He asks her something only Phoebe has ever bothered to. He asks, "What's your dream outcome, being back here?" He asks like he really cares about the answer. She doesn't have to think much harder about it to know this, right here, is what makes him so easy to talk to.

So, she tells him: "I've always been the only girl. My dad's got two sons. Noah, who left home as soon as he could, because he wanted to be his own man. He never wanted a legacy handed to him. The only thing my dad is more than he's disappointed in him is... proud. He's so proud. Abel and I don't expect the Noah treatment. Noah's the first born. Eldest child. All kinds of privilege happening, but he's not even a jerk about it so we can hate him. Abel takes it on – but he just doesn't want to disappoint him too. Doesn't want to be the ungrateful kid with cold droves of green money lining his pockets, just to turn around and tell our dad he couldn't care less about a medical supplies business. I guess I want to – be considered." She's never talked to anyone but Phoebe about this. Even then, never so extensively. Emily feels her nape heat with that realization. It makes it her turn to be self-conscious. "Is that pathetic?"

Were she a little more tipsy than she is, Emily suspects it would have left her tearing up, the fervor with which Alex insists, "*No.* Emily, no, it's not pathetic at all."

She nods slowly. Absorbing it, the faith he has. Her fingernails scratch softly through fluffy orange fur. "I hope not. It feels that way a lot. If my dad still doesn't take me seriously after this fundraiser... I think it's best that I'm done here. Back to the city."

Chapter Four

EMILY

Everything that week had gone smoothly. Like puzzle pieces, Emily had thought, until circumstances turned it into an array of fallen dominoes on an otherwise calm Friday morning. Just like that: One down, and the rest damned to follow.

It comes in the form of an innocuous-looking envelope. When she opens it, she finds the ivory, textured card paper of the RSVP invitations the entire guest list had been sent a fortnight ago. This one is from Mr. Fogleman, which was why Emily couldn't wait to open it. His was one of the names at the *top* of the guest list, and for good reason.

Over the years, there were a great deal of adjectives she had applied to herself. But she's never been overconfident. At least, she'd thought so. As she looks down at the RSVP invitation, with its *'NO, SORRY TO MISS IT!'* option sporting a cavalier, blue-inked checkmark beside it, she isn't so sure anymore.

There was a selection of contingency plans that came along with planning an event. Back-up plans in the event of an act of God or an error of man; from thunderstorms to someone pulling the fire alarm. For all of those, Emily had notes in her folder. Yet she hadn't seen this coming. That made this disaster, and that's *exactly* what it is, not only unprecedented – but also unmitigated. Her temples throb with anxiety that makes a weapon of itself.

Emily doesn't have to consult her notes to know Mr. Fogleman has never before missed a function hosted by *Harrison Health*. Not until it's her who's cajoled the reins out of her family's hands, having sworn up and down that she can handle it. *I've got it, Daddy,* she'd insisted. The only thing she's got right now is tears in her eyes, blurring her vision and rendering it as twisted as it all feels.

"Emmy?" Abel's voice punctures Emily's haze. She turns to look at her brother with a sedate look. He looks so much like their father in old photographs, only with their mother's eyes. *What is she supposed to say to him?* "What's wrong?" he asks immediately. She has no right to be stung by that question. Somewhere in her mind, Emily knows it.

Does it matter that her pride recoils at the assumption, if she's already proven it right? The heart knows no reason. She's known it since she was young.

"I—" her voice breaks, undeniably. Grabbing her coat, she practically runs out of the house. "Gotta go! Meeting!" she hollers over her shoulder, in an uncouth way her mother had raised her never to do.

Her mother had also specifically raised her not to interrupt a man's work. Yet here she is: standing in Alex Carter's classroom. There's a brown paper bag in her hand, within which she's brought along... a bribe. She doesn't outright say she's waited for his free period, but there's too much telltale bashfulness staining her cheeks anyway.

Alex being who Alex is, only looks delighted. Winded, astonished, worried—but just delighted, at first. Emily offers a meek, pathetic wave. "I brought you a croissant."

"You felt that bad about the cafeteria food we get?" Alex quips. With the way his eyes pore over her, questioning and concerned, she knows it's only for her benefit he does it. It makes her feel as big as a gnat. "We have vending machines, too?" It comes out in a question. He sounds so tender, Emily nearly bursts into tears. Instead, she can do her version of it these days: she takes a deep, shaky breath. The bag crinkles noisily when her fist tightens around it.

She holds it out to him before her nails burrow holes through it. He comes to her and takes the bag—but the other set of fingers curls around Emily's wrist. He gives it a questioning squeeze, his eyes wide and bloodshot up close. "A major donor pulled out. We aren't going to meet this goal. If my family was underestimating me before, this just proves them all right. I officially have no leg left to stand on." Distressingly, Alex smiles at her a little helplessly. Emily emphasizes: "I'm *legless,* Alex."

He's never touched her this casually. Even a few days ago, when she'd been tucked in on his couch and talked to him for hours, then been demolished at a too-competitive game of Scrabble, his hand had only brushed hers once. He'd almost jumped to the other side of the couch after that. Now, his hold traipses from her delicate wrist to her hand, which his cocoons. "You have great legs. You just may have tripped. Come sit. We can figure it out. What else are beck and call boys for, boss?"

Emily's smile feels watery. But it's one she means. How could anyone not? The man's hands settle on her hips and lift her onto his desk with a surprising amount of strength. Emily can't remember the last time she genuinely *yelped.* He sets her down with a small smirk on his lips. Unfortunately, he steps back and puts space between them. Emily can think of at least two ways he could've made her feel better... but he's talking. There is a splotch of ink staining his knuckles. Her skin heats at her subsequent train of thought.

"Do you want my opinion?" he asks candidly.

"I wouldn't have come back to high school if I wasn't in dire need of it."

Alex nods to himself. If he was a cartoon with a thought-bubble over his head, Emily thinks, it would be overflowing with words. He takes the moment to pull the croissant out of the bag, and tear it into two pieces. She doesn't miss that he hands her the fractionally bigger one. She doesn't have the energy to think about the way that makes her want to cry, too.

She stiffens twice as dramatically because of it when he says, "I think... you should talk to your dad. There's no world in which he doesn't have a million contacts with piles of money, Em. He could easily help replace the donor. No one would even know. Just you, me, him—"

"—and *Mr. Fogleman,*" Emily spits scornfully. "But I can't. You know I can't, Alex. Everyone already thinks I'm stuck at *Take Your Daughter to Work Day*, and it's going to look exactly like that if I do. He already things I'm just a dumb girl, in over my head. This would be basically hammering the last nail in. I have to be a real grown-up!" His face does that thing again. Emily hisses, "*Stop* looking at me like that!"

Alex flinches as if she's struck him. "What am I looking at you like?" he asks woundedly.

All she can manage is bitter grumbling, "Like I'm *cute*."

"You are cute, though," Alex huffs. She didn't know before today how, when he's frustrated, he runs his hands through his hair. It almost looks like he's pulling at the strands. "You're beautiful. And smart, and hilarious, and brave. And really, really cool. But – you're also being a little immature right now. Real grown-ups don't call themselves that. Nor do they lead with ego. This is bigger than just proving yourself to your family. There's real people you're helping. Don't let your pride be a hurdle that keeps you from helping a real cause."

Emily has to put down the croissant, then. She buries her face in both hands. "I sound like a spoiled brat, don't I?" she mutters, pressing her hands against her face as if the weight of her shame could hide her from the truth. She doesn't have to look at Alex to know he's grinning at her again.

***

She can't hold off for long. It takes her till noon – but Emily finally forces herself out of her car, and through the pristine doors of *Harrison Health*'s imposing building. For a company that deals with such an unglamorous trade, no one can tell when confronted by the display of tinted glass and chrome. When she had been a little girl, Emily really had come to work with her dad. This building had been her version of a princess' castle. Back then, there hadn't been a question of which of the three Harrison children most belonged here.

Her glossy black pumps click-clack their way through the marble hallway, and several heads turn to look at her now. She can only hope they're mostly looks of admiration; she'd donned a power suit for this meeting, making herself a vision in a white suit and black blouse with buttons like pearls, and her hair halfway swept up but not secured too severely. She doesn't turn back to check.

For most of her life, Ward Harrison, chairman of Harrison Health, and her beloved father, had spent most of his time in this place. Much of that time period, their family had grown familiar with his stout, stern secretary, Ingrid. Emily's mother sent Ingrid's family Christmas presents every year. Somehow, it's Ingrid who nods at Emily—and her ensemble —with what she interprets as approval. It's the most Ingrid ever offers, the tiny quirk of her lips she gives Emily, before she says, "Go on in, honey. I didn't tell him you're the meeting. He'll be thrilled."

Emily grins. The stamp of approval from Ingrid meant more than one from just about anyone else. Anyone but the man behind the executive desk, who rises to his feet the second she steps across the threshold. "Mr. Harrison," she says, and can't help but join her dad when he starts laughing at the formal address.

"Princess," her dad guffaws. He smokes too many cigars too unapologetically. His voice is gravel by now. "To what do I owe the pleasure?"

"I'm your one o'clock. Please sit? I'm here for a meeting, not—" She isn't off to the best start, gesturing broadly. It isn't articulate. Her knuckles blanch from her hold around the handle of her briefcase. "Please, Daddy?"

Emily hates that her dad still looks more amused than anything. Like he's just humoring her. He probably is. There's a part of her, more than anything else, that needs to wipe that look off his face. So, she admits, "Mr. Fogleman isn't coming. An RSVP came in this morning."

Her father's smile does dissipate. But he hardly looks stricken. Then again, this is who she knows him to be. He's unerringly good-humored, and unflappable besides. His features betray nothing. When he gestures her on, it doesn't look desperate or lost. "Go ahead," he instructs, in complete control.

"I didn't come to ask for a handout," she says and, by God's good grace, manages to keep from sounding as defensive as she feels. "I did my research. If you look in this binder—" Emily pulls a folder out of her briefcase, this one definitely sans any whimsical vision boards, "—or the USB drive inside of it, I've included a formal summary of the fundraiser's goals. Our current projection, factoring in Mr. Fogleman's absence. I've gathered intel for potential new sponsors, and a revised budget. I'm here for *advice,* Dad. Because I love you, of course, but I've always respected and admired your business acumen. Who better to seek expertise from, right?" Somehow, her voice remains steady all the way through. Her hands, too, settling in her lap after she's handed it all over.

Her heart holds up, even as she watches her father go through her work in front of her.

His face gives nothing away. For a long, endless slew of minutes, he only reads, making the same muted humming sound Emily herself makes sometimes. A lifetime seems to pass. Emily isn't certain she's grown at least three new grey hairs in the meantime.

But then he says, "I can see that you've put a great deal of thought and work into this, Emily." It's so rare for her father to simply say her name, it has her sitting up straighter in her seat – if that's possible, at this point. "Why don't we go over it together? Let's see how we can make it work."

ALEX

Just like that, it's the day of the fundraiser. It had been many days and epiphany since Alex had set foot on the Windham estate. Today, he returns in a rented tuxedo to a place with the same bones yet an entirely new outfit of its own. He should've known. Sophie Davis had made a household name for herself back in the big city before she'd relocated to Maplewood Grove. Her soul was calmer than ever, she'd told him. But she hadn't lost her touch.

Just walking in through the massive, heavy oak doors, one is met with an archway. What a production it is: bedecked in white, twinkling fairy lights and silver, glittering flowers. Cutouts of snowflakes hang from the ceiling, by some thread so thin it is almost invisible to the naked eye. They sparkle, but not with glitter. It looks like raindrops, if raindrops were crystallized in a moment in time. The cool-toned decor is offset by soft amber lighting. At sporadic but artful distances, sleek ivory candles are upheld in holders as antique as the bones of the mansion, swathed in sparkly swathes of taffeta. There are tables that dot the sprawling ballroom, too, covered in white linen tablecloths that boast iridescently glittering netting over the plain sheets.

It's a fairytale come to life. Alex doesn't know how ethical it is to think, seeing his students scattered around the room with shimmering black waistcoats: *Does this make them my dwarves?* A couple of them are taller, if not as tall as him. Thanks to whatever they're feeding today's kids.

No matter what, it feels serendipitous. It feels ideal – *right*.

Just the place to ask Emily Harrison out.

There had been a speech. Alex knew there had been a speech. It's just that... Emily walks into the room, and he forgets how to speak. Well, he forgets how to *breathe*. The sight of her in the rich emerald velvet of her gown is worth more than breath, anyway. Swept inward from either side, it cinches at her waist, teasing with a slit that starts at the middle of a creamy thigh. Alex can feel his mouth go dry.

Of course, she walks right up to him. Gone is the panic shrouding her features from yesterday. She glows– her skin sun-kissed beneath warm lighting, as if there's a light inside of her that doesn't turn off. "Woah," he blurts, making a fool of himself.

She looks thrilled by his lack of control. "Thank you. You look pretty dapper yourself."

For a moment, Alex genuinely things the cover of *Can't Help Falling In Love With You* has begun to play inside of his head. It isn't until Sophie's voice hollers from the corner, "Test out the music before people show up!" She nods eagerly, leaned back into Liam's chest. Alex wants to turn into a puddle. His face probably resembles a tomato.

But then Emily's teeth are scraping over the full curve of her maddening bottom lip. Almost shy as she asks, "Do you want to?" As if there is a planet on which the answer wouldn't be *yes*. He isn't a man who takes liberties—but his hands make a point, reeling her into his chest, his palm skirting up her arm, cradling the back of her hand in it. Her breath is shaky against his throat. She smells like roses and cinnamon.

This. This would be the moment to say it. To ask her out, to quit being a coward, to put things in motion and make his intentions known. All he can do is hear his pulse roar in his ears, and try to keep his legs from giving out when the hand not holding his curves over his shoulder.

Chapter Five

ALEX

For better or for worse, their impromptu slow dance hadn't lasted long.

Half an hour later, the room is packed.

He takes on the task of supervising students, making rounds from those doing coat-check duty to those manning the raffle. He'd shooed Emily away. He'd *insisted* she go enjoy this event she'd worked so hard to organize.

Now, he can't stop chasing her around the party. No matter where he winds up, she remains in his peripheral view. And what a sight she is. All the townspeople are dressed to the nines. Alex hadn't grown up with the kind of wealth the Harrisons and Bakers had—but even he can see the difference. With the way he's been spending time with her, he'd almost forgotten she's from this world. She's warm and down-to-earth; so grounded.

It takes seeing her in this element to understand it's one of hers.

Her eyes land on him like she's heard his thought out-loud. A beat later, she's gesturing him over. His feet don't give him the moment to consider it. They're already on the move. "This is Alex," Emily is already introducing. Not for the first time, her arm hooks through this. It feels different when there's a diamond bracelet around her wrist.

"That's me," Alex agrees, refusing to let his restless hands reach for a collar that feels too tight all of a sudden. Like she can sense it, her hand covers his, twining their fingers. "He's one of my co-hosts. Without him and Sophie Davis, I couldn't pull this off— Yeah, you've already met her. She looks like a Disney princess, doesn't she?" She's charming and kind. Keeping it light, even when her stance means business.

One wouldn't know she carries stress in her shoulder till the fancy couple slips back into the party crowd and Emily's shoulders drop. Her forehead presses to his shoulder. "I think we might pull this off, Alex."

He doesn't bother stopping himself before his cheek comes to rest atop her head. "You didn't have to do that, you know?" He feels her nod more than he sees it. "I know," she murmurs. "I wanted to."

When she's off again moments later, Alex makes a beeline towards one of the long tables to the side laden with finger-foods and beverages; another option to the ones circulating on trays through the party. The tables are manned by Noah and Hannah. Alex already knows... The refreshments weren't what lured him over.

Noah doesn't pretend otherwise. It's rare to see his usually bright, boyish grin flattened to a firm, pursed line that looks too much like Emily when she's thoughtful. "You've been avoiding me, dude," he says bluntly. More fact than accusation.

"I have feelings for Emily," Alex replies. It's a minor miracle that his heart doesn't just stop in his chest. He isn't sure how, but he isn't questioning it. "And I hope you can be okay with that, man. You're important to me. I love you like a brother. But I think I could fall in love with this girl. I'm already falling. And for what might be the first time in my life, I've got to do it. Even if it isn't the easy option."

Noah quirks a single brow at him. His features slack in a way that makes him look older than he typically does. Somewhere amidst their exchange, Hannah has slipped out of sight. *No close witness if he's going to kill me,* Alex deduces. Except, Noah says, "Why shouldn't it be easy?"

"Because I'm—" Alex fumbles. Noah rolls his eyes, and it reminds Alex of Ethan.

"You're a good man. If she feels the same about you, I can't imagine a happier ending. But I do appreciate your candor," Noah says. To Alex's ear, it sounds... a little off. A little too formal for how Noah speaks.

It takes a moment for realization to dawn. When it does, it takes Alex's eyes from narrowed, suspicious slits to wide-eyed recognition: "Ethan and Olivia already told you, didn't they." It isn't a question.

Now, Noah chortles. "Sure," he agrees. "But I also have eyes."

EMILY

There were only two people with whom Emily had shared her secret vision board: Phoebe, from whom she kept no secrets, and Sophie, who'd turned her vision manifest. It's exceptional. The kind of exceptional, Emily thinks, that defies the want of approval.

How could she need validation when it's so clear what a success this is? Her dad had come through. Instead of meeting their target, the fundraiser, only an hour and a half in, is slated to exceed it. This community, the very one she'd been so fearful she'd have to give up, has come through. With more support than in her wildest dreams.

Dot Simmons, she expects. The mayor and Loretta, too. But the turnout is outstanding; everyone has shown up. Together, they are evidence that it doesn't have to be buckets of money. Sometimes, a lot of people in a community could come together, and bit by bit, make an astronomical difference.

"Maybe it's the lights and stars, Sophie," Emily squeals, her hands in Sophie's as she twirls her around giddily, "but everything is falling into place." Sophie throws her head back and laughs her full laugh, and there's a knowing gleam in her eye that Emily doesn't look away from.

"I think something real could happen," Emily whispers. "With Alex."

Sophie beams wider, if possible. "Finally. I bet on you against Liam at *Thanksgiving*."

It's one more piece falling into place on this enchanted night when her father makes his way onto stage. There isn't a big one. Truthfully, Sophie and Alex had said there likely wasn't need for one, and Emily had almost gotten rid of it entirely. But there's a spot. When he's already there, the spotlight making the streaks of silver in her father's dark hair look honey-toned, Emily can admit: she'd wanted this.

She watches his hand wrap around a microphone, and feels her chest puff with pride as his gravelly voice fills the room. "Good evening, ladies and gents," he greets. "We're so thrilled you all made it. It's a special night for a special cause. Community, you all know, is built brick by brick. Surely none of the success of tonight would be possible without you. Or—" he pauses, but somehow the effect doesn't feel dramatic with him; only enhancing, "—without my little angel of a girl, Emily Harrison. She put hours of work into getting this night to this point." Applause overtakes the room. Emily's face flushes with pleasure.

Her eyes take in the room. They catch on Alex's, a few paces away from her. He looks right at her when he claps. His gaze is so warm, Emily can feel it like a caress. She almost misses her father saying, "And when she needed help, she wasn't too proud to ask her old man to step in and save the day. It really does take a village, y'all. That's what Harrison Health is. Thanks for all your support."

It's only when her hand reaches to shield her face—as if she can hold fast to the dregs of her dignity so long as no one sees the heartbreak on her face. Her fingertips come away wet, stained with mascara she hadn't bothered to ensure was waterproof.

Well, she supposes it's fitting that she look the way she feels. Even younger and stupider than she'd set out to prove she wasn't.

Chapter Six

EMILY

I should've never come back. It runs on a loop inside her head. She can barely see through the film of tears that spill, and spill, and spill...

Emily has no choice but to stop when she collides with a wall. Except it isn't a wall. It's Alex—his warm, solid chest that his frantic hands attempt to reel her to. Petting her. Trying to *comfort* her. "Don't go," he begs. Emily squirms away. She doesn't need his comfort. She doesn't *want* to need his comfort.

His fingers graze her cheek, and a sob wracks from her chest. Harshly, Emily wrenches away. "I just want to *go*," she cries inconsolably. Every cell in her body can feel the eyes on her. She's making a spectacle of herself. No, maybe just a joke.

Alex seems to think it is the best moment to say, "I think you should talk to your dad, Em. Tell him how you feel. Maybe he'll s—"

She thinks she hears it, acutely. The sound of her heart freezing in slow-motion. "Oh, do you?" she asks icily. She doesn't give him a chance to say more. She sees his mouth open, and she cuts in: "Well, thanks for the advice. I know you're so much older and wiser, or really think you are, but I'm not one of your students and I'm already suffering from the *last* piece of advice you gave me."

ALEX

Never privileged in the same way half the people in this room are, but Alex has rarely felt wronged in his life. It was a different kind of privilege. But, as is often the case throughout history, it isn't until a privilege is stripped away that one appreciates its significance.

For all that Emily taunts him with his age, he feels about five years old, arguing, "That isn't fair!" Like she's his mother and has confiscated his Nintendo for halfheartedly doing his chores. "Don't treat me like an emotional punching-bag. Please, Emily. I'm only trying to help."

"I didn't *ask* for your help!" she almost shouts.

Alex is stunned still. "He's wrong. You know he's wrong. All you have to do is be brave and tell him. How can he see you're grown up if you don't show him?" He can see it in her face—all over it—the moment his words sink in. All they elicit is hurt. Emily is forceful when she barrels ahead, shoving past him.

His hands tremble with panic. He doesn't think—he *can't think.* His hand catches hers before she's slipped away, and reels her back with a tug. His muted grunt is lost to the recesses of her mouth when his covers it. Alex pours his heart into it, and all his pleading. The fickle organ lodges in his throat when she shoves him off, shoves him *away.*

"*Are you kidding me?*" Now, Emily does shout. Her face is flooded with color; red marring her cheeks viciously, only worsened by tarred streaks trailing from her swollen eyes to her raw cheeks. "What's wrong with you? You can't— Not *right now*—"

"I have feelings for you. I—Em, please. *Please?* I'm falling in love with you. I want to date you. Then more than date you. Just—" He's begging. He doesn't care if he has to beg.

Except Emily looks agonized. "I can't," she chokes out. Her hands are shaking, too. The way her lip does. He doesn't think she realizes it, the way she's inching away, even as she speaks to him. "This is too much... I can't *do this* right now. Do you—Can you understand?"

There's nothing else to do. He shoves his hands into the pockets of his jacket for both their sakes. "I can wait," he tells her. "You're worth waiting for."

Emily nods frantically. Mostly, she just looks relieved that she gets to go. How far will she run away, once she gets going? Alex could swear her fist is wrapped around his heart. That doesn't feel like a metaphor. Every step she takes away from him, he feels a twinge in his chest. It all hurts. "But don't go. You– Just stay, okay? I'll leave you alone. But you have to see this night through. You owe it to yourself. You owe it to this wonderful cause, and Sophie. You've worked too hard. No matter what your dad says. Em, this success belongs to you. The townspeople came for *you*."

She keeps nodding as she disappears out of sight. Whether he got through to her or not, Alex doesn't know. He doesn't get to, just now. His mouth tastes like her lipstick—and it doesn't feel like he'd dreamed it would.

He doesn't know what he'll do, if this is the last he sees of her. If this is the last kiss he gets to give her, when it was the wrong one. All these weeks of worrying, of panicking and overthinking and twisting himself into knots, and the only thing that matters might just be ruined anyway.

What was he supposed to do now?

"Sir, I'm— Hello. I'm Alex. Carter," he announces. As he was cutting his way through the throng, he'd imagined this going a little less feebly. His voice was supposed to be booming. There should have been a crowd around Ward Harrison, looking on, intrigued and nervous, while Alex launched into his monologue. Equal parts heart-wrenching and scathing, of course.

Instead, the man is standing in the corner, scrolling through his phone.

It isn't like Alex doesn't know he's kind of a passive person. He's never been the sort of person who put much stock into the pains of being misunderstood. Whatever life gave him, Alex found a way to deal. Apparently, it only stood to be true when it was about him.

All it took was approximately seven minutes of just standing there, thinking harder and harder about the tears rolling down Emily's cheeks. Thinking about the look of absolute devastation on her face when her father's speech had taken a turn for the worst. And he couldn't stand it. He couldn't stand to just *think* about it any longer.

"Mr. Harrison?" Alex says more forcefully. This time, the man's head snaps up. His brows only making it halfway to intrigued. *I'll take it,* he thinks. "Can I talk to you? I– Well, I worked with Emily on this. And I want to say some things to you I think she needs to, but isn't brave enough to do yet. But... Sir, she's special. She's a special girl—" he lets out a vague, strangled sound. He doesn't wait for the man to go anywhere with him. Here, apparently, is where they are going to do this. *All right.* "Woman. She's a special *woman.* Maybe the *most* special woman. And I know you're a big, powerful man. You're very successful, and from everything *both* your children say about you, you deserve every bit of that success. But I think you're doing yourself a disservice. No, I know you are. You're doing your big, fancy *company* a disservice by not bringing her on board."

The man says nothing. Alex fears he just may be sick on the man's shoes. They are probably made of Italian leather, or something equally overpriced. For a moment, Alex imagines he's only been standing here and staring at the man, and his whole, semi-triumphant speech has only come to pass inside his head.

Then, Ward Harrison's rumbling, authoritative voice drawls, "I'll take it under advisement, Alex Carter," before he simply walks away.

Epilogue

IN THE END, it isn't because of Alex that she doesn't leave. Or rather, doesn't *entirely* leave. It's for Sophie, who truly has worked too hard, for Emily to be so disrespectful as to just leave. She winds up just outside the doors of the mansion; her body nearly collapsed against a pillar—and a cigarette between her teeth.

This is how her father finds her. When he does, he cloaks her shoulders in the thick wool of his coat. Emily would sass him, but she can't think of a single clever thing to say. She isn't even sure just opening her mouth won't result in another bout of tears. Who knew what he'd think of her then?

It's the most rebellious Emily has been in years, when she takes a hearty drag from the cigarette between her teeth, and exhales smoke right at her father. As close to acknowledgement as he's going to get. Much to her frustration, a corner of his mouth rises. "Filthy habit, you know," he harrumphs. Right after, he plucks the cigarette from between Emily's fingers and takes a hearty drag of his own. Mingled with his exhale, he asks, "Do you want to work at the company?"

Just when Emily had been sure she had nothing left to give to this day, her father manages to elicit shock so robust, it nearly tips her over. "What."

"Emily, you heard me."

Just once, and maybe spurred by nothing short of bitterness, Emily pettily, "No, I don't think I did, Dad. I heard your speech inside, though. Since you're the one saving the day, what would even be the *point?*"

There's enough heat to the words, at least, for him to pivot towards her. "I want you to stay. I want you to sit on the next meeting, and share your ideas with me. I just wish you'd have told me. I don't understand why someone else had to announce it to me." He doesn't apologize for his speech. Then again, Emily didn't expect him to. She hadn't expected any of this.

She's just exhausted enough to admit: "I didn't want to have to, Dad. I wanted you to see me. Without having to beg for your considera-tion. Abel and Noah never had to."

It's a more graceless sound than she's ever heard her father make. But he actually *snorts* into a chuckle. "You look so much like your mom, Em, I sometimes forget how much like me you are." He shakes his head at her, laughing more—somewhere down the line, it makes him cough. He hands her back the cigarette with a soft smile. "Monday morning, 8 AM sharp. But for tonight, I think you have something more pressing. That young man over there—he's ready to slay a dragon for you. Maybe it's time you let him."

She doesn't have to ask who he means.

This once, she listens to her father. Never mind her pride. Or rather, never mind it after she's fixed the streaks of ruined makeup across her face. Thankfully, it isn't difficult to find Alex. He's standing by the refreshments table, handing out punch to a group of teenagers. His mouth is smiling, but his brow is crumpled. Emily only waits long enough for the crowd to dissipate before she comes up behind him, planting a furtive palm on his elbow.

"Hi."

Alex looks at her like she could knock him over with a feather.

She hopes he'll make a better deal with gravity when she proposes: "Before the lights go out, maybe we should finish our dance." It's not unimpressive that he manages to nod. He even looks completely adamant doing it. When his hands are steady, steering her to the middle of the room, and falling into a stance that would have done well at cotillion, Emily is sure he can take it. She tells him, "I didn't need you to rescue me."

Alex sounds a little defensive, arguing, "I wasn't trying to rescue you! I was trying to..." Emily nudges the soft jut of his chin with the tip of her nose, like a bird coaxing her babies. "Help. I just wanted to help. It hurt my heart to see you hurt. Maybe I was rescuing myself, in a roundabout way."

"That's so cheesy." Emily can't help but laugh. After everything that had happened in the last hour, she can't entirely believe she can still laugh. But Alex makes her.

"Do you... like cheesy?" he asks. She hates the caution lancing its way through his features. The Alex she knows is open and honest.

"I like *you*. I've always liked you. But it just isn't the same way, now," Emily rants, and barely notices that, somehow, they've stopped swaying. "I loved fairytales growing up. But I have grown up. I don't need any true love's kiss waking me up, saving me from some tragic slumber. I can slay my own dragons. If anything, I'm looking for a noble steed, or whatever. A sparring partner. Something more even."

Alex's mouth lingers at her brow. Pointedly, he cajoles her body back to swaying. "What if... just this once, we tried a true love's kiss... just because?" he whispers, his breath warm against her temple, the weight of unspoken promises hanging between them.

Her heart nearly stops. But, for how tender her words are, there is nothing shy about them. "I don't know. I've never had one before," she says. He rears back. This close, in this light, Alex's eyes are the darkest Emily has ever seen them. "Maybe we should try it. Let's see. And I'll... tell you how I like it."

They're both already smiling when their lips meet. It isn't a privilege people often consider, to get a second kiss. The first can be an impulse as easily as it can be a choice. The second kiss, though—that comes with knowledge. It may boast a certain intimacy. It roars like a fire, and a feverish pulse, between them now. That intimacy.

It doesn't break off for a long time. There is a different song filling the room when they finally do. A fresh chorus is the backdrop when

Emily sighs, "I'd say it's got 'happily ever after' potential." Their third kiss only confirms it.

The End
Did you enjoy Small Town Moments?
Please consider rating it on Goodreads, Bookbub, or your favorite retailer. Reviews help me reach new readers.

Want more Maplewood Grove romance?
Small Town Memories, Maplewood Grove - Volume 2

Join my newsletter for updates and giveaways!
www.daisylandishromance.com

About the Author

Daisy Landish is a clean romance and cozy mystery author whose clean and sweet novellas have tugged at readers' heartstrings around the world. When she's not writing love stories, Daisy spends her time reading, hiking at dawn, and riding into the sunset on her horse, Rosebud.

Join Daisy's Newsletter for updates and giveaways!
www.daisylandishromance.com

facebook.com/daisylandishromance

x.com/daisy_landish

instagram.com/daisylandishbooks

amazon.com/author/daisylandish

bookbub.com/authors/daisy-landish

goodreads.com/Daisy_Landish

Also by Daisy Landish

Clean Regency Romance

The Lady Series - The Allington Collection

The Lady Series - The Gillingham Collection

The Lady Series - The Blackmore Collection

The Lady Series - The Norrington Collection

Clean Contemporary Romance

Timeline Retreats - Romcom

Maplewood Grove Series - Small Town

Love on Spruce Island

Second Chance

Cherry Tree Island

The Wedding Trio

Extra Credit

Counting on the Cowboy

Focusing on the Cowboy

Mistletoe Magic

Grounded at Christmas

Cozy Mysteries

Sophie Brooks Mysteries

Jane and Kennedy Daniels Mysteries

Pine Grove Mysteries

Annie Archer Paranormal Mysteries

Wilma Wade Holiday Mysteries

Mike and Maddie Mysteries

Mystic Moonhaven Mysteries

Sweater Weather: Cozy Mysteries for Fall

Summer Vibes: Cozy Mysteries for Summer

Let it Snow: Cozy Mysteries for Winter

Spring Break: Cozy Mysteries for Spring

www.ingramcontent.com/pod-product-compliance
Lightning Source LLC
Chambersburg PA
CBHW020837260626
47169CB00003B/1033